# SOMETHING TO LIVE FOR

## Whiskey Mountain Book 4

### Samantha Baca

# Contents

# <u>One</u>

## Paisley

"Can I help you?" I asked grumpily, my foot tapping impatiently on the floor as Maverick lowered his head and approached the counter. I had done well with ignoring him this week, but we were shorthanded today, so I agreed to handle the register for a while until Calli caught up on orders in the kitchen. Of course, he just had to pick today to stop in for food. *Fucker.*

"Yeah, can I get the chicken and waffles?" He grinned a dimpled smile, his stupid voice deep and sultry.

"No." I glared at him and then leaned to see past him. "I can help who's next."

"Really?" He cocked his head to the side as a smirk graced his full lips that had once devoured mine.

"Paisley," Calli hissed, bumping my hip with hers as she walked past me. "Stop it."

"I'm not helping him." I folded my arms over my chest and raised an eyebrow at her.

"You're on the clock, which means it's your job to help *everyone* who comes in," she replied with gritted teeth. Thankfully, she was my best friend and needed me more than I needed this job, but I knew my attitude wasn't making things any easier for her.

"Fine." I turned my head, my eyes narrowing as they

found his. "Chicken and waffles with extra spit. Can I get you anything else to eat?" I forced a smile on my face, pretending to give the best customer service I could muster.

Calli sighed heavily as she walked over to the other register and called the next person up. It was a good sign that we were finally catching up and the rush was coming to an end, but that meant Maverick had no real pressure to move through the line now.

"What are my options?" he asked softly as he licked his lips.

"There was a dead cat out back in the alley. I can see if Frank can get it on the grill for you."

"That's not the kind of *cat* I usually enjoy eating."

I felt the heat flush through my skin as I looked down and jabbed the order into the computer.

"$17.37," I said, keeping my tone clipped.

"I thought it was the lunch special for $12.99?"

"I added a brownie."

"Oh. Okay. I wasn't really in the mood for a sweet treat, but why not."

"It's for me."

The corners of his lips turned up into a devilish smile as he passed his credit card.

"Well, in that case, why don't I take you to dinner tonight? I'll gladly buy you more than a brownie. Something more *filling* and *satisfying*."

"No thanks. I'd rather take my chances on the brownie and my vibrator leaving me fulfilled and satisfied, if you know what I mean. At least I know they won't flake out on me." I winked and held my hand up as I pretended to whisper but said it loud enough for Calli to hear. She had already cleared the line, so at least I didn't embarrass her in front of any customers.

Maverick let out a long, heavy breath and locked eyes with me.

"I'm sorry that I had to cancel our date."

"Which one?" I replied curtly.

"Fair point. I'm sorry that work has been so busy and that I've had to go out of town so much on such short notice. I didn't mean to upset you by canceling so much. Trust me, I was looking forward to it as much as you were."

"I seriously doubt that."

"Then give me a chance to prove it to you. Have dinner with me tonight."

"No."

He rubbed his lips together, unsure of what to say as I passed his credit card back to him.

"Your order will be ready in a few minutes. You can wait over there for it."

He nodded and lowered his head as he walked off. My insides felt like they were on fire as I fought off the flurry of emotions that were storming inside me.

"What the hell was that?" Calli asked as Maverick left with his food.

"Nothing."

I grabbed the towel and began wiping the counter down, even though it was clean from when I did it five minutes ago.

"Bullshit."

"We were supposed to have a date last weekend, and at the last minute, he had to cancel. It wouldn't have bothered me so much, but it was the third time in two weeks. I'm just over it."

"What happened to you being so obsessed with him?"

"I guess constantly being pushed to the side will do that."

"But you liked him," she pressed.

"Yeah, and sometimes things change. It's not a big deal, Calli. Let's just let it go and get through the rest of the day."

I walked off and hated the nagging feeling that told me she was right. I had liked him, but none of that mattered if he didn't like me enough to make an effort to really get to know me.

# Two

## Maverick

"How long do you think we'll have?" I asked, pressing the phone to my ear as I took a bite of my food. I didn't technically have time to stop for lunch, but Paisley had gotten so deep under my skin by not answering my texts that I made it a point to stop in and see her today.

"Two, three weeks tops. That storm is coming sooner than we expected."

"Alright. I'll shuffle some stuff around and get a crew out to finish the job in Claremont. After that, we have one more to do in Fallen Oaks, and then I plan to slow down some for the winter. Send me over the details, and I'll approve everything tonight."

"Will do, Boss."

I hung up the phone and took a drink of water, washing down my food.

Business had been busier than usual lately, with all of the new shops opening in Whiskey Mountain. On top of that, I had taken on a lot of jobs outside of town to help my cousin while he recovered from injuring his back. It had been more than I could chew, but I did my best to keep my head above water until things slowed down. The nice thing was that even though we were headed into winter, HVAC work never stopped, so I didn't have to worry about pulling in more business during the slow months.

What I did worry about was getting Paisley to talk to me and better yet, to give me a second chance to take her on a date. I'd finally gotten up the nerve to ask her out, only to have a slew of unexpected things thrown at me to the point I had to cancel after trying to reschedule several times.

Paisley wasn't like other girls, and I knew that. That was what attracted me to her the most. Any other girl would be jumping at the opportunity to have me take them out, but Paisley was far from giving in any time soon. *If* I was going to get the chance to take her on a date, I was going to have to work hard for it—which I kinda looked forward to. I was accustomed to hard work and going after the things I wanted, which meant getting Paisley's attention was no different.

I threw my trash away and got back to work, ready to wrap up a few jobs so I could finally stop and breathe.

By the time I got home, it was already past nine and I'd gone all day with only stopping to eat lunch. I grabbed a slice of leftover pizza out of the fridge and scarfed it down, not bothering to warm it first. I wanted to take a shower and relax but found myself reaching for my phone instead.

**Me: I know you're still mad at me, but I just wanted to say you looked beautiful today.**

I didn't expect Paisley to respond, so I set my phone on the charger and hopped in the shower. When I came back, there was a new text message waiting for me.

**Paisley: Unsubscribe.**

My cheeks split with a grin as I shook my head and climbed into bed. Paisley might just be the death of me, but what a way to go.

The next day, I got up early to get a head start since I was starting a new job on the outskirts of town, and there was a snowstorm moving in. I wasn't sure how bad it would get, but I didn't want to get caught in it and not be able to get home before it hit.

When I pulled up outside of the general store, I took a look at the old, worn-out building and sighed. The owner had informed me that they would be closed for a few weeks while they worked on renovations inside, though the outside needed a facelift as well. It surprised me that they were even willing to put so much money into fixing up the place, given that there were at least three other general stores in town that were easier for people to get to. It didn't make sense to me to fix something up that wouldn't get a lot of traffic, but that wasn't what I was hired for.

I climbed out of my truck and headed inside, shivering at the chill already in the air. A few guys were finishing up painting the walls while Mr. Crawford sat in front of the register, watching. I'd met him a handful of times, and while he looked rough and rugged on the outside, he was one of the kindest people I'd ever met.

"How's it going?" I asked, nodding to the workers as I stood beside him.

"It's looking good. The store needed an update, and Clara said that yellow and gray were the new popping colors. I don't know about it, though."

I scrunched my face and looked at the paint sample cards in his hands.

"Which wall are they painting yellow?" I asked, looking around the store at the gray and white walls that hadn't been painted yet.

"The one right behind me." He jabbed his thumb over his shoulder and shook his head. "She said it wouldn't hurt to have a little bit of sunshine behind me when people come to talk to me."

I chuckled and took the cards from him.

"Is this the yellow you're going with?"

"Yup. Sunny Side Up."

I held it against the wall and then leaned back to see it behind him.

"I think it'll look good."

"Yeah, like sunshine coming out of my ass. Maybe we can put a rainbow up and I can tell the kids I farted that out."

I shook my head and laughed, enjoying the way the corners of his eyes wrinkled as he grinned. He was ornery, but that was what I enjoyed the most about him.

"Did you decide on whether you wanted to go with another swamp cooler or if you wanted to try refrigerated air?"

"Clara wants the refrigerated air, but I told her that we could save that money and go to Italy someday before we die."

"What did she say?"

"She would rather be cool on a hot summer day than sit around and wait for my old ass to take her to Italy."

"So, then we're doing the refrigerated air?" I asked, my lips turning up in a smile.

"Nope. She can be hot and moody, as usual. I promised her when I proposed that someday we would go on a romantic getaway to Italy, and I've never lied to her yet. We'll go with a new swamp cooler, and she'll just have to get one of those little neck fans I see people wear at the baseball games."

"You're a good man." I clapped him gently on the shoulder. "Do you mind if I get started and take a look at what we're working with?"

"Not at all. But that storm is moving in quickly, so I don't know how much time you'll have. I'll need to close up early so I can get home before I get stuck here, and I imagine you'll want to do the same."

"Not a problem. I would like to take a look at the heater so I can get that working for you again. I don't want you to be stuck without heat while they're finishing the rest of the renovations."

"Thankfully, most of it is already done. Plus, once that storm hits, I won't be able to get in here for a while. The roads get covered in ice, the snow piles up in the blink of an eye, and it takes forever to get the roads cleared out here. I was planning on being closed the rest of the week due to the storm anyway. I know most of the guys won't be back until after the roads clear, so don't stress yourself about trying to work a miracle with that heater."

I nodded and looked around the store. A lot had been done already, but I didn't want to drag this job out for a few weeks since I had others lined up. If I could get the heater up and running, then at least I wouldn't have to worry about him being here in the cold. I could always come back later to get the swamp cooler set up since it would be a while before he would need it.

I was so focused on figuring out what was wrong with the heater that I hadn't noticed everyone else had left for the day until I went into the store to see if Mr. Crawford had a flashlight I could borrow. He was standing by the register, stuffing the newspaper into his bag when he lifted his head and smiled at me.

"All done?" he asked.

"Not yet, but I think I figured out what's wrong with it. My flashlight died so I was coming to see if you had one I could borrow."

He reached beneath the counter and pulled one out.

"I need to head home before the snow gets much worse. I worry about Clara being by herself and trying to start a fire. I know she can do it, but I like to take care of my lady."

"Okay," I said, nodding though my mind was still going a mile a minute about fixing the heater.

"I don't want to leave you by yourself to lock up, but I can see that you're not ready to go yet. I can leave the keys with you if you want to stay a little while longer to work on that damn heater, but I wouldn't stay too long, or you'll risk getting stuck here."

"Are you sure you don't mind?" I didn't want to make him uncomfortable with leaving me alone in his store, but if I could have at least twenty more minutes to work on it, I could possibly get it up and running for him.

"I don't mind one bit." He handed me the key after taking it off of his keyring. "But you get yourself out of here before you get stuck. These roads back here aren't anything to play around with."

"Yes, sir."

"I'll get in touch with you next week, and we can see where everything is. Be safe heading home."

"You too. My goal is to get it up and running here in the next thirty minutes if I'm lucky."

He nodded and then pulled on his wool cap before heading out into the storm. I knew that I should probably be smart and leave with him, but I also couldn't stand the thought of him coming back before I could and being stuck in the freezing cold with no heat in the place.

# Three

## Paisley

"You want me to get what?" I asked, gripping the steering wheel tighter as the snow fell in a heavy blanket around me. My phone was in one of the cupholders on speakerphone so I could hear Calli.

"They're these cute little Thanksgiving gnomes. Clara said I could have them to decorate Cravings before the holiday, but I needed to go by and grab them. I don't think I'll get over there before this storm hits, and since you're already headed that way, I thought maybe you could pop in and grab them. She's not at the store, but Mr. Crawford should be."

"Gnomes?" I questioned, a shiver running through me. "You know how much I hate gnomes, Calli."

"I know, but these ones are cute. They're holding pumpkins and have rosy cheeks. They're so adorable."

"You're lucky I love you."

"Does that mean you'll go get them for me?"

"Yeah, but only because I'm already headed that way. But you owe me. It's freezing out here, and I just want to get home so I can curl up in front of the fire with my fuzzy socks and read a dirty book."

"I'll buy you new fuzzy socks and more smut books for doing this for me. Just send me the links to the ones you don't have yet."

"Deal."

"Be careful and let me know as soon as you get home. Okay?"

"Will do. You be careful, too. This storm is insane, and the weather report on the radio a few minutes ago said it's only going to get worse."

"Yeah, I'm closing early and heading home to check on Mom. I'll let you know when I get there."

"Sounds good. Talk to you soon."

I didn't bother to press the button to disconnect the call since I was too focused on the road I could no longer see in front of me. Calli hung up, and a few minutes later, the store came into view. I put my SUV in park and rushed inside, hoping the gnomes were already waiting for me.

I knew the place was being renovated, but I didn't expect it to be so eerily dark and quiet.

"Hello?" I called, walking through the front of the store and peeking down the aisles. "Mr. Crawford?"

I couldn't imagine that he was just hanging out in the store with the lights off, but I hadn't been in here before, so I had no idea where his office might be—assuming he had one. I kept walking, going up and down the aisles as I struggled to listen for any sounds of movement.

Just as I was getting to the last aisle, I rounded the corner and smacked right into someone coming out of a narrow hallway.

"Holy shit!" I gasped, clutching my hand to my chest as the blood rushed through my ears.

"Hey, are you okay?"

Strong hands wrapped around my waist, the intoxicating

scent of soap and cologne filling the air around me.

"What are you doing here?" I demanded as I looked up and found Maverick looking me over.

"Working. What are you doing here?"

"I came to pick something up for Calli." I pulled out of his grasp and stepped back. "Where's Mr. Crawford?"

"He already left for the day."

I rolled my head on my neck, the frustration mounting quickly.

"Okay. Did he by chance say anything about some gnomes he was leaving for me to pick up?"

"He did not."

"Great. Looks like I came all this way for nothing."

I turned on my heel and headed for the door with Maverick right behind me.

"Maybe you came to see me."

"Nope."

"Well then, maybe it was destiny bringing you here knowing I would be here."

"Again, nope. It was gnomes. Stupid Thanksgiving gnomes that Calli asked me to pick up that aren't even here. A wasted trip out here for nothing when I could already be home by the fire, warm and toasty."

"Do you want me to follow you home to make sure you get there safely?" he offered, though I didn't hear any flirting in his tone. He looked past me to the storm raging outside, concern heavy in his eyes. The snow was still coming down in sheets, but the wind was intense as it howled around us.

"No, I'm fine, but thank you. There's nothing my four-wheel drive can't handle—"

Before I could finish my sentence, there was a loud cracking sound as snow flew in the air. We rushed to the window to find a large tree had been knocked down, likely due to the weight of the snow on it combined with the forceful wind pushing it over.

"I'm gonna venture to say that it can't handle that," Maverick said with a heavy sigh.

I stared at the parking lot and our vehicles that were now trapped beneath the tree.

"This seriously cannot get any worse," I muttered, pinching the bridge of my nose and closing my eyes.

"I mean, it could, but the good news is that at least we're stuck here together," he offered.

"You think that's *good* news?" I arched an eyebrow and glared at him.

"I think it's destiny forcing you to give me another chance."

"You've had your chances, and you chose not to do anything with them." I folded my arms over my chest and stared out the window, wondering if there was any way I could get the stupid tree off of my car and safely drive it home. There was a massive dent in the roof and I wasn't a tree expert or anything, but my guess was that this one weighed at least a couple hundred pounds. It looked like his truck had taken the brunt of it, but there was still damage to my car.

"Well, it looks like fate has decided to give me another one now that we're stuck here together."

He rocked back on his heels, smiling smugly as if this wasn't the worst thing in the world that could happen to us.

# Four

## Maverick

I wouldn't necessarily call being stuck in a snowstorm with Paisley hell, but apparently, that's what it was when she called Calli and told her that hell would have to freeze over before she would consider being nice to me. I knew most women thought I was hot but devilishly hot was a whole new level, and I was ready to show Paisley just how devilish I could be.

"Well, you're not getting your gnomes, and who knows how long it will be before I get out of here," she said into the phone, pacing the small space in the aisle.

I had already told her that there was no point in calling for help because everyone in town had already turned in for the day. Even Mr. Crawford hadn't answered my call when I tried letting him know we were stuck here. Unless it was an absolute emergency, no one was going to risk coming out here to save us. And being stuck in a fully stocked general store wasn't such a bad thing. We had access to food and running water, and once I had a chance, I planned to get the heater up and running. Sure, we didn't have a comfy bed to sleep in, and there was no way to start a fire if we got cold, but things could be a hell of a lot worse.

"Yeah, I tried calling, but they said no one would come out to take care of the tree until the roads were cleared. I'm hoping that means a day or two tops." She looked up at me and glared before turning and walking down another aisle.

I knew Paisley didn't want to be stuck here with me, but

I was feeling quite thankful that I finally had a chance to talk to her without her running away. Sure, I would have to hide anything she could use as a weapon against me, but if I could just get through that icy wall she'd built, I knew I could find the Paisley I had gotten to know and was quickly falling for.

I browsed the back of the store where the camping supplies were kept while Paisley finished her phone call. So far, I had grabbed a few flashlights for when the power went out—which I expected would be any moment, given how much the wind had picked up, and a double sleeping bag for us to share. I knew that she wouldn't be ecstatic about sleeping next to me in the same sleeping bag, but it was the best way to share body heat to keep us as warm as possible. I also grabbed some hand warmers and extra blankets since we wouldn't have any heat tonight.

"So, what is the plan?" Paisley asked, hand on her hip as she stood above me.

"I'm getting the stuff we'll need for tonight and thought we could set up in the breakroom. It's the smallest space in here, so it'll be the easiest to keep warm."

"Are you supposed to be helping yourself to everything?"

"Yes. We're stuck here whether we want to be or not. My only focus right now is keeping both of us from losing a limb to frostbite. We have no way to get out of here to get the resources we need. Therefore, I'm utilizing what's available to us."

"That's stealing," she scoffed, shaking her head.

I stopped what I was doing and stood up, my body painfully close to hers. She sucked in a breath, her eyes widening when I invaded her space, easily towering over her petite frame.

"It's not stealing if I intend to pay for everything. I've

known Mr. Crawford for years and know that he would want us to use what we need. I've already started a list of what I'm taking, and then I'll settle with him once we're able to get out of here."

"I guess it's not bad if it's just a day or two worth of stuff."

"Try weeks."

Her eyebrows shot up on her forehead as she stared at me in disbelief.

"This is day one of the storm, Paisley. We haven't even had the worst of it yet. No one is going to risk their lives to deal with that tree until it's safe to do so. We have food, water, and a dry, safe place to sleep. We'll be just fine."

"You think that we'll be *just fine* spending weeks cooped up together in here? I don't think so."

"We don't really have much of a choice, now do we? Instead of standing here, throwing a fit, why don't you find something for us for dinner? Nothing that has to be cooked because we're limited to a microwave, and the power is probably going to go ou—"

Paisley gasped loudly as the lights went out, leaving us in darkness. I grabbed one of the flashlights, turned it on, and handed it to her.

"Go figure something out for us for dinner," I instructed, knowing that she needed me to be firm with her right now. She was frightened, and I understood it. But I needed her to get on board with things or it was going to be a long, dreadful time stuck together.

# Five

## Paisley

"You've got to be kidding me," I grumbled as I struggled to get the flashlight to sit right on the small counter space in the breakroom so I could see what I was doing.

"Need help?" Maverick offered, startling me.

"No."

I knew I would eventually have to give in and stop being so mean to him, but right now wasn't the time. I just wanted to go home, get comfy in my warmest pajamas, and sleep in my own bed. Instead, I was stuck with him for who knew how long in a general store without power or heat.

"Eventually, you're going to have to get over hating me so we can work together as a team," he said softly, his hand brushing against my lower back as he grabbed the flashlight and held it for me.

"Not today, Satan."

His chuckle vibrated through the air as I worked on cutting the blocks of cheese into bite-sized pieces. There wasn't any fresh produce, which left us with few options for dinner. I had decided to do a mini version of a charcuterie board and grabbed a few packs of different cheeses, lunch meat, and some assorted crackers. I knew it wasn't much, but it was the best I could do for now.

I tried to ignore the way my body automatically wanted to

lean into his or how I could feel the heat radiating from him. I had been cold the moment I got into my car earlier and still hadn't warmed up. I didn't have high hopes for tonight, given we had no power for the heater to run, nor could we safely start a fire.

"Do you want something to drink?" he offered as I finished cutting the last few pieces of cheddar cheese and laid them on the paper plate.

"What are the options?"

"Bottled water, milk, soda, beer, or wine. There might be juice in the other cooler. I didn't go that far to check yet."

"Wine," I answered quickly, hoping it would warm me up.

He arched an eyebrow at me and then nodded, handing me the flashlight before heading back into the store.

"Aren't you going to ask what kind I want?" I called after him.

He stopped and popped his head back in through the doorway.

"You only drink sweet wine unless you're drinking a glass with dinner, and then you'll drink red, but only if you're having steak. You don't like dry wines and can't stand anything that fizzes," he said matter-of-factly. "I hate to break it to you, Pais, but this is a general store—not a winery. Your options are going to be limited and the selection an assortment of cheap wine. I'll do my best to pick something that *might* meet your *constantly changing* expectations."

My jaw hung open, my mind processing his words as he disappeared as quickly as he appeared.

*Did he just get snarky with me? Was he insinuating that I was hard to please?*

I moved the charcuterie plate to the rickety table in the corner of the room and sat down. It wasn't fancy, but it would have to do.

The room was bigger than I expected, though I knew that would change as soon as we put down the sleeping bags and had to share the space—which I still wasn't looking forward to. A few weeks ago, I would have been balls to the walls excited about being snowed in somewhere with Maverick. But a lot had changed since then. Okay, so *feelings* had been hurt since then. My heart was angry with him, but my vagina was flashing a "now open" sign because she was stupid like that. I blamed it on the soft, lingering scent of his cologne floating through the air, making my head even more confused and foggy. He did smell good, though.

"This is the best I could find," Maverick said, setting the bottle on the table and taking a seat.

"Thank you." I reached for the bottle, but before I could grab it, he pulled it away.

"Na uh." He shook a finger at me, the bottle firmly in his grasp.

"Are you holding my wine hostage?" I cocked my head to look at him. I narrowed my eyes and leaned into the dim light of the flashlight, making sure he could see the glare I was giving him.

"Yes. Until you stop being so mean to me. I said I was sorry, and I meant it."

"Doesn't mean I forgive you."

"Then let me work for it."

"For what?"

"Your forgiveness."

"And how do you plan to do that?" I rested my arms across

my chest, more so to keep warm than to look annoyed—but it helped.

"However you want me to." He pulled his chair in closer to the table and slowly unscrewed the lid. It was definitely a less expensive bottle, but I loved that we didn't have to worry about finding a corkscrew to open it. The convenience outweighed the cost or quality of the wine right now.

"I know that I let you down by having to cancel our dates repeatedly, and I feel terrible about it. But I was trying to help my cousin while he was in a bind. It wasn't like I purposely chose him over you, Paisley. I was trying to do the right thing, but in hindsight, I can see that it also meant that I was hurting you, and that was never my intention. This may come as a surprise, but I don't chase after women. Never had to. But, as you can see, that's all changing with you."

I sank back against the chair and exhaled heavily. Calli had mentioned that his cousin needed help, but I didn't ask for any details. It didn't really matter because I couldn't fault him for helping his family, no matter how much I wanted to. Plus, he just admitted to being willing to chase after me, which was insanely flattering.

"So, you tell me what I can do to earn your forgiveness, and I will."

He spoke softly, the dim light casting a warm glow over his features as he grabbed a disposable cup from the coffee bar and opened the bottle.

"You don't have to earn my forgiveness," I replied with a sigh, earning another arched eyebrow from him as he poured.

"I feel like this is a trap," he teased, handing me the cup.

"It's not. I mean, I'm still mad at you, but it's nothing you have to be forgiven for. That's a bit drastic, especially considering that we're not even dating or anything."

"So, you're just going to stay mad at me until you decide you're not mad at me anymore? And there's nothing I can do to fix it in the meantime?"

I shrugged and took a drink, enjoying the sweetness on my tongue. I felt more comfortable staying mad at him, even if it was over something that now seemed so silly. But I wasn't willing to put myself out there again and risk being the one to get hurt if things didn't work out the way I wanted them to between us.

"I'm just saying we might be stuck together for a while. It *might not hurt* to clear the air between us so we can try to make the best of it." He offered me a sympathetic smile.

"Can I ask you something?"

"Of course."

"Why do you keep saying we might be stuck here for a while? Why not a few days?"

"Have you ever spent a winter in Whiskey Mountain?" he asked, cocking his head to the side.

"No, but it can't be that bad."

His face softened as he waited for it to sink in.

I closed my eyes and let my head fall forward.

"It's going to be *that bad*." I groaned, finally acknowledging the reality of our situation.

"Now you see why I want to make the best of it. A few weeks stranded with someone can really change your perspective about them." He grabbed a small piece of cheese from the plate and popped it into his mouth while I felt any remaining hope I had left drain out of me.

24

# <u>Six</u>

## Maverick

"I have good news and bad news. Which one do you want first?"

Paisley was still sitting at the rickety table with her legs pulled up against her chest as she finished her second glass of wine.

"I'm honestly surprised to hear that there could be any good news at this rate. Let's start with the bad, I guess."

"Okay, the bad news is that I could only find one sleeping bag." I held up the bag to show her, trying to keep my face from giving away that I was lying to her.

"What's the good news?" Her brows pinched together as her body stiffened.

"The good news is that it's a double, so it's big enough for us to share."

Her face went through a flurry of emotions before deciding on anger, her green eyes blazing.

"I'm not sleeping with you."

I pulled my shoulders back, took a deep breath, and slowly let it out. Now wasn't the time to fight with her, especially since it was getting late and I was already exhausted from the past few days.

"Relax, Paisley. It's not like I'm going to fuck you senseless and give you multiple orgasms in it. Regardless of whether you like it or not, this is where we're sleeping tonight. Once I get the air mattress blown up, I'll set this up, and we can go to bed."

"You can sleep in there all by yourself," she said bitterly, standing up and heading toward the door.

I stepped to the side, blocking her path as my hand shot out and wrapped around her waist to stop her.

"Trust me when I say you don't have a choice in the matter," I warned, my voice low and gravely. "The power is still out, which means we don't have any heat options other than this sleeping bag and relying on each other's body heat. So come hell or high water, I will drag your stubborn ass back to this sleeping bag if you attempt to leave. I would appreciate it if you would just stop being difficult because it's been a long fucking day, and all I want to do is get some sleep so I can figure out the next steps tomorrow."

Her body froze against my touch, her breaths soft and shallow, though I could see the vulnerability in her eyes.

"Fine, but if you so much as touch my ass in your sleep or if I wake up with a cock pressed against it, I'm cutting your balls off."

"Trust me, if you wake up with anything against your ass, it'll be my tongue."

Her face darkened in the dim light as she blushed and looked away.

I grinned a smug smile she couldn't see as I headed back into the store to grab the air mattress. When I came back, Paisley was finishing sweeping the floor and had pushed the chairs against the wall to give us more space. It was such a small room that it almost made me feel claustrophobic, but I took comfort in knowing we would stay the warmest in here, given how much colder the rest of the store had been when I went in to grab stuff a few minutes ago.

Once everything was set up, I pulled the top cover back and motioned for Paisley to get inside. She rolled her eyes and shivered as she climbed in.

I might have lied when I told her this was the only sleeping bag there was. There were a few other ones on the shelf, but this one was the thickest and looked most promising. Plus, there was something comforting about knowing that Paisley would be next to me so I could keep an eye on her and make sure she was okay. If we did individual sleeping bags, I wouldn't be able to do that as easily and would probably lose an eye if I looked over to check on her.

I climbed in beside her and pulled the top over us. I had been able to find a few pillows, so I added those, hoping it wouldn't be terribly uncomfortable for either of us.

"Are you comfortable?" I asked.

"Mmm hmm," she mumbled through chattering teeth.

Without considering the consequences first, I reached over and grabbed her, pulling her back flush against my chest.

"It hasn't even been two minutes," she grumbled, pulling her hips away.

"Relax, Paisley. This isn't an attempt to try to have my way with you. I can hear you shivering from here, and I'm not about to willingly let you lie beside me and freeze. I run hot, so I have plenty of heat to share."

"Are you seriously making this about how hot you are?"

"Yes, because it comes in handy. And if for some reason we don't make it through this, you can say you went out cuddled by one of the *hottest* men in Whiskey Mountain."

I totally meant it as a joke, but her head whipped around as panic filled her eyes.

"You think there's a chance we won't make it?"

I reached up and pinched her chin between my fingers to keep her gaze on me. I needed her to look me in the eyes as I said it and know that my words were true.

"I promise you we will, Paisley. I just need you to trust me and allow me to take care of you the way I need to."

She nodded her head slightly, not bothering to break the physical contact between us. Maybe this was the fresh start we needed.

# Seven

## Paisley

I woke up with a rock-hard cock pressed against my ass.

While I wanted to be mad at Maverick for it, I knew it was out of his control as he snored loudly, completely unaware of his *little friend,* locked and loaded, fully prepared to storm my gates. Only he wasn't little—not by any means.

I shifted my weight slightly, trying not to wake him up, and unintentionally grazed his cock harder. I froze for a second, ignoring the heat that rushed between my legs at the promise of a good time behind me. If he was already this hard without trying, I could only imagine how hard he could get when awake.

I wanted to press my luck and see if I could get him there, but the last thing I wanted was for Maverick to wake up and catch me. I still wasn't ready to let go of the anger façade I was carrying, even if he had the kind of cock that wet dreams were made of.

My back arched as I attempted to stretch, pressing my ass further down on his erection. Almost immediately, strong hands reached out and grabbed my hips, stopping me from moving any further.

"What are you doing, Paisley?" he asked, voice still thick with sleep.

"Stretching," I said, half lying, half telling the truth. "Why? Am I bothering you?"

"You know damn well what you're doing, and you're doing it on purpose."

"So, what if I am?"

I suddenly felt bold, the pressure building between my thighs too much for me to think straight.

"Is that your way of torturing me? To prove your point?"

"No," I breathed out, wrapping my hand over his until he relaxed his grip on me enough to allow me to press my ass over his cock again. "But it turns out there is a path to forgiveness, and it's a little bit south of where you're currently at."

"Fuck," he hissed under his breath as I lowered his hand to where I desperately wanted it.

"Are you sure about that, Paisley?"

I nodded my head against his chest, eyes closed as I waited to feel his touch.

He pulled my hair to the side and kissed along my neck, sending shivers up my spine. Maybe *this* is what we should have done last night to stay warm because my body was on fire.

His palm flattened against my stomach as his fingers inched their way down under the waistband of my leggings and skimmed the top of my panties.

I held my breath as he continued kissing my shoulder, his touch electrifying. The heat from his skin radiated through the thin fabric covering my pussy, making me ache with need.

"Your pants are really soft," he said, catching me off guard as he shifted from slipping his fingers inside my panties to rubbing them against the inside lining of my pants.

"Thanks, they're fleece lined. I get cold easily."

"Those will come in handy out here. The winters get bad. Definitely softer than wearing thermals, but those really help keep you warm as well."

"Umm, Maverick?"

"Yeah?"

"While this is all very informative, my pussy is going to explode if you don't touch her in the next twenty seconds."

"Well, we can't have that happen, now can we?"

His breath was hot on my skin as he chuckled and nibbled my earlobe before pushing my panties to the side and running a finger through my slit. A hiss rushed through my lips before I could stop it.

I didn't bother answering him as I closed my eyes and leaned into his touch. His fingers glided effortlessly through my wetness as he brought me closer to climax. I wanted him to roll over, crawl on top of me, and own my body, but he didn't. He stayed behind me, teasing me with his cock that I wanted—no, *needed* inside of me.

"Mav—" I started to object right as his fingers found my clit and began rubbing just the way I needed. Before I could get my words out, he was sending me over the edge as my pussy spasmed with the best orgasm of my life.

32

# Eight

## Maverick

"Where are you going?" Paisley asked as I stood up and stepped around the air mattress without tripping in the small space.

"I want to get a head start on the heater since the power is back on. It'll take time to warm things up, so it's better to get going."

"How about finishing with the thing you already got all hot and bothered?"

She rolled onto her side and stared at me, that same vulnerability in her eyes that I saw yesterday.

"As much as I would love that, Pais, it's not going to happen."

"Why not?" Her head pulled back in surprise as anger flickered in her eyes.

"Because as much as I would love to fuck you senseless, I'm not touching you again while you're still mad at me."

"Fine—I'm not mad anymore. There. Settled. Let's go."

A smirk tickled the corners of my mouth as I tried to hide it.

"I'm afraid it doesn't work that way."

She took in a harsh, deep breath and blew it out, clearly indicating her frustration with me.

"It could—if you weren't being so *difficult*."

"I'm not the difficult one, Paisley. You're the one who's been mad at me, remember?"

"Yeah, and I just said I was over it. So what's the big deal? You're just doing this to punish me."

"No, I'm not. I'm doing this because I'm not going to take advantage of you being horny now, and then you regretting it later when you remember that you're mad at me. When you're ready to talk things out, I'll listen. Until then, sex is off limits."

"You'll finger me until I come, but sex is off limits?" she countered snarkily.

"Exactly."

I winked as she opened her mouth to spout off a sarcastic response before closing it. I could stand here and fight with her all day, or I could get my ass in gear and get the heater working. I turned and grabbed my tool bag from the floor before heading out to get to work.

A few hours and several curse words later, I had the heater up and running again. I made a note of the things that I would need to come back and fix later, but for now we had heat. I put my stuff away and then went in search of Paisley.

It wasn't like there were many places for her to hide, yet it felt impossible to find her. I went down every aisle of the store, calling her name but not getting a response. Finally, I went back to the break room, hoping she was just hanging out in there, only to find it empty.

Just as I was getting ready to call Dylan to see if Calli had heard from Paisley, I heard water running in the bathroom. I let out a long sigh and leaned against the wall, wondering what in the world she was doing in there.

I raised my hand to knock but waited as I heard singing on the other side. I didn't want to interrupt her and have her stop, so I stood there listening like some creeper as she belted out a popular love song. She had a beautiful voice, which wasn't surprising given everything about her was beautiful. Even her attitude when she was mad at me—though I would never openly admit that.

I leaned against the wall, enjoying the next song until she stopped abruptly, and the door swung open.

Paisley walked out, wearing nothing but a smug smile as if she knew I had been standing there the entire time.

"You've got to be kidding me," I groaned under my breath, closing my eyes and resting my head against the wall.

"You're the one who said sex was off-limits," she replied nonchalantly.

I heard her footsteps as she walked past, making sure to keep my eyes closed so I wouldn't be tempted to change my stance on the no-sex rule.

# <u>Nine</u>

## Paisley

It was much colder than I expected, especially since I was prancing around naked without a care in the world.

I wanted to show Maverick what he was missing after his whole *no sex until we talk* speech this morning, but I hadn't stopped to think whether there were cameras in the store and if my little antics were being put out there for all the world to see.

It wasn't like I had clean clothes to change into, so I grabbed my hoodie and slipped it on before heading into the store in search of something to wear. Freshly laundered clothes were out of the question at this point, but I had noticed a small section of clothing when I was wandering around earlier—before I got the wild hair to attempt to *shower* in the bathroom and strut my stuff. However, I didn't know if you could technically call it a shower when you were forced to use the cold water from the sink and ended up splashing around like a wild bird. Thankfully, I had found a razor so I could at least shave, even though my skin immediately prickled from the cold, so it was rather pointless on my legs.

As I walked down and browsed the aisles, I found there was an odd selection of stuff, and I couldn't quite figure out what kind of store it was supposed to be. There were plenty of groceries and household essentials, but there was also an entire section that felt geared toward wilderness survival, which could come in handy. I recognized the air mattress and sleeping bag that Maverick had put together for us last night, then frowned when I saw the assortment of single-person sleeping bags on the same shelf.

"I was hoping you wouldn't see that," he said, nodding to the shelf where I was looking as he rocked back on his heels next to me.

"Why? So I wouldn't know what a big liar you are or because you didn't want to get caught making up stories to get me to share a bed with you?"

"I did lie about there not being any other sleeping bags," he admitted with a shrug. "But I knew that if you had the choice of sleeping next to me or on your own, you would have chosen to sleep on your own."

"Surprise, surprise. I wonder why, *Pinocchio*." It wasn't his nose I was worried about growing right now; it was the cock he was purposely withholding from me, leading to my increased frustration.

"I did what was best for everyone last night, Paisley. You don't have to believe that, but it's true."

"And how was lying to me about there not being any other sleeping options the best for everyone?"

"Easy. By us sleeping in the same sleeping bag, it kept us warmer than we would have been sleeping on our own. Our shared body heat was essential given how cold it got last night."

"Yeah, and you having your cock pressed against my ass this morning was just a bonus for you?"

"No, but shoving it in your tight little pussy would have been."

My cheeks flushed with heat as I looked away, not wanting him to see the effect his words had on me.

"What were you looking for?" he asked, changing the conversation.

"Something to wear," I answered with a heavy sigh. "I don't want to wear the same stuff every day, but it's not like there's a laundromat close by. Not that I want to wear clothes from the rack that haven't been washed either, but beggars can't be choosers."

"The sink in the bathroom should be big enough to wash stuff in small batches. They have laundry detergent over there, and I think I saw some rope we could use to make a line to hang everything while it dries."

"That could work," I said, thinking it over. "I think I saw some T-shirts over on the other side of the store. I can grab a few, that way I have something to wear while I'm washing the rest."

"Let's go check it out." He smiled and walked off, leading the way down the aisles.

It felt weird shopping when there was no one else in the store, but it felt even stranger to be living in the store for the time being.

Maverick and I shopped the limited clothing options, and I cringed when the only underwear they had were full on granny panties. I set my pride aside and grabbed a pack, knowing no one was going to see them anyway. Maverick grabbed a pack of plain t-shirts and a few pairs of sweatpants, calling it good. I didn't question why he didn't need underwear because I couldn't stand the thought that his junk was just hanging around freely. That would be a slippery slope that I had no right to be on.

Once we had what we needed, we went to the small bathroom and crammed ourselves inside as he worked on plugging the sink before adding some detergent to the water. It wasn't big enough to do a lot at once, but being stranded in the store meant we had all the time in the world to get our laundry done.

I grabbed the clothes I had been wearing yesterday and

added them to the water before discreetly pulling my panties off and tossing them in. The lone thong swam alongside my new grannie panties, probably wondering what in the world those hideous white things were.

Without batting an eye, Maverick grabbed them and swished them around in the water as if he wasn't standing there washing my panties.

"You don't have to do that," I whispered, looking down into the water to avoid meeting his eye.

"It's not a big deal, Paisley. They're just panties. Besides, my fingers have already been inside your pussy, coated with your arousal, and felt as you spasmed against them as you came. Washing them is the least offensive thing I plan on doing. You know, once you're not mad at me anymore."

Heat spread throughout my body as I watched him grip them tightly in his hand as he squeezed the water out of them before plunging them back into the water. As much as I tried not to, I couldn't help but imagine his hands grabbing my ass the same way he was currently manhandling my panties.

# <u>Ten</u>

## Maverick

"What do you feel like for dinner?" I asked, sitting down in the cramped space at the table in our temporary room.

"That's not a fair question because everything I could possibly want isn't an option," Paisley said with a sad-sounding sigh.

"What is it that you want?"

"I would kill for a steak and baked potato."

"I can make that happen."

"Oh yeah? How exactly are you going to do that? There's not even a stove, and while I hate to burst your bubble, I don't think microwaved steak is going to be very appetizing. Plus, I've looked inside that thing, and I don't think I would trust cooking anything in it." She shuddered and wrapped her arms around her legs, pulling them to her chest as she sat on the air mattress.

"No, you're right. The microwave is out of the question. I did, however, see an air fryer that we can use."

"Where?" Paisley looked around the small room, and I grinned, loving how cute she looked.

"They don't have one in here, but I saw some on the shelf. I can add it to my tab, which I technically needed a new one anyway."

"You don't have to do that. Not for me. I don't want to be the reason you rack up a lot of debt here that you wouldn't have if I weren't with you."

"Relax, it's not that big of a deal. Plus, it's not racking up a lot of debt. We're buying stuff we need, and I refuse to live off cheese and crackers for a few weeks until someone can clear the roads out here."

"Excuse me, *Mr. Fancy Pants*. Those cheese and crackers were delicious."

"Yes, they were. You make a very tasty charcuterie board. But you even said it yourself that you were craving something else."

"Okay. Fair point. But don't talk shit about my cooking."

"I won't. But that means you actually have to cook," I teased. "Cutting up cheese and putting it on a tray with crackers isn't cooking."

"You better watch yourself before I cut *you*," she warned, green eyes dancing with humor.

"Promises, promises." I shook my head and stood up. "Come on, let's go pick stuff for dinner."

I held my hand out to help her up and then looked away when I remembered she was still wearing just a hoodie while waiting for the other clothes to dry. She had been covered up with a blanket, but now that she stood there with long legs leading up to heaven, I couldn't remember what I was supposed to be focused on.

"Was there something else you wanted to eat?" she asked coyly, batting her eyes playfully as mine finally made their way back up her body and landed on her face. She chewed her lower lip, which was already moist from her licking it a few seconds before.

"Yeah, there is, actually," I answered, wrapping my arm around her waist and pulling her against me. A gasp escaped her plump lips as her eyes widened. Her chest rose and fell heavily as her body reacted to my touch.

I allowed my hand to fall from her waist and gently brush against her ass before I moved it in between us, painfully close to her bare pussy. She arched her back slightly, taking a small step as her feet spread apart, allowing me to feel the warmth radiating from her body.

All I had to do was lift my fingers a fraction of an inch and I could feel the wetness that was pooling between her legs. I could slide my finger inside and fuck her with it until she came again like she did this morning. But I wasn't ready to keep fucking around with Paisley, not until we cleared the air between us.

"Yeah, I think I'll cook some chicken too." I nodded my head as if I had just made the biggest decision in the world and turned to head into the store. I didn't stop or look back at Paisley as she cursed me loudly because I knew if I did, that would be the end of me. I would be balls deep inside of her within seconds, and there was no coming back from that.

# Eleven
## Paisley

That fucker.

# Twelve

## Maverick

Paisley had been mad at me for at least an hour, hissing at me every chance she could get. Which, in all fairness, I didn't mind. I kinda liked the feisty little demon she was acting like because it would be that much better when I fucked it out of her.

The clothes were still wet, so she was running around in the hoodie that seemed to be getting smaller by the minute. Either she was purposely pulling it up to drive me crazy with glimpses of her ass, or it was so cold that it was literally shrinking like my balls would when I attempted to shower later.

I had picked out food for both of us after she refused to help me earlier. I knew she was mad at me for teasing her, but then again, she didn't *have* to wash all of her clothes at the same time. She could have found a pair of sweatpants to put on but had decided to tease me by showing me what I was missing out on. The problem was that I was a man and Paisley was a woman I had wanted for a long time, which meant my resolve was quickly fading.

Cooking the steaks in the air fryer was a new experience for me, but thankfully, I had found some seasonings and was able to figure everything out. While I might have lied about needing a new air fryer—especially since I had no idea what to do with it—I was pleasantly surprised that this one had two large racks so I could cook the potatoes at the same time, as well as a handy booklet with tips on how to cook everything.

I wasn't sure how she wanted her meat cooked, so I went with medium, knowing I could throw it back in if she preferred it well done. Right now, if I had to go based on her temperament, I would have just thrown it in for a few seconds and then called it good so I could offer her the blood of an innocent animal as some sort of sacrificial offering.

"What would you like on your baked potato?" I asked, hoping she would at least make this part easy since it was her food at stake.

"Just butter and cheese if we have any."

I felt my lips curl into a smile, thinking about how we still had plenty of cheese, thanks to the blocks she had cut up for dinner last night. I had grabbed a small container of butter earlier to cook the steaks with and then decided to clean out the fridge so we could use it now that the power was up. It was more or less clean, aside from some take-out containers that needed to be thrown away—nothing like the microwave that was sure to give me nightmares.

"Dinner will be ready in a few minutes," I replied, cutting the potato open and moving my fingers away to keep from getting burned by the steam. "The steaks are medium, but I can cook yours longer if you'd like."

"Medium is perfect. Thank you."

I nodded my head, unsure if she could see me, as I worked on finishing the potatoes. This wasn't how I would have envisioned myself making dinner for Paisley, but then again, I hadn't imagined getting stranded with her, either. Had Calli not sent her for the gnomes, I would have been stuck here by myself with far less to keep me entertained.

I plated our food on the paper plates I'd grabbed from the store and set them down on the table. Paisley had already set some bottles of water on the table for us—or at least I assumed one might be for me—who knew with how she was glaring at me right now—and a bottle of wine. I didn't bother to ask if she needed a glass for it, given that I didn't want to lose an eye as she picked up the steak knife I had given her and stabbed the meat with it.

At this rate, I was going to be leaving here with a fully stocked kitchen and new appliances with how much stuff I was casually borrowing and adding to my tab. But if there was a way to make things a little easier while we were here, I was going to do everything I could.

I cut into my steak, giving her a few minutes to get some bites into her before I attempted to start a conversation. I was learning so much about Paisley in such a short time, but I had yet to find a part of her personality that I didn't like. Even when she was angry—that turned me on the most, yet I wasn't willing to dive down that rabbit hole to question why.

She lifted her fork to her mouth and bit the piece of steak off, closing her eyes and moaning softly as she chewed. I tried to look away, but her features pulled me in, keeping me locked in another trance as I watched her eat.

"Oh my God, this is so good."

Her eyes fluttered open and landed on mine. I took a bite and held her gaze, not bothering to let her see how affected I was by her compliment or the tender meat swishing around in my mouth. *Also—holy hell, why hadn't I ever used an air fryer before? That thing was pure fucking perfection and 90% less work than grilling.*

"So, why are you mad at me?" I asked, getting straight to the topic we needed to discuss as I shifted in my seat and took another bite.

She raised an eyebrow and glared at me under her thick lashes as she looked down to cut another piece of steak.

"You really want to do this *now*?"

"It's not a matter of what I *want*, Paisley. It's a matter of this conversation is happening—right here and right now."

She set her fork and knife down on her plate and folded her hands in front of her on the table while giving me the coldest expression I had ever seen. Normally, this kind of behavior would have me zooming out the door and not looking back. But with Paisley, it made my dick twitch.

"So, what, you think I'm just going to tell you because you've *demanded* it of me?"

I lowered my fork and knife to my plate and steepled my fingers in front of me as my gaze locked onto hers and held it. The way she shifted in her seat and how her breathing changed didn't go unnoticed by me.

"No, we're going to deal with this because we're two powder kegs one spark away from exploding. I refuse to fuck you until we've cleared the air between us, Paisley, but that's getting harder to do. So, for the love of God, we're going to deal with whatever this is between us so I can bury my cock inside of that tight little pussy of yours and fuck it like it's begging to be fucked."

Her jaw dropped open for a split-second before she composed herself and pulled her shoulders back.

"I feel like I put myself out there by letting you know I was interested in you. Then you canceled our dates repeatedly, and that made me feel like I wasn't worthy of your time since you kept choosing to do something else instead of what we had planned. I know you've said it was work-related, however, I don't know whether to believe that or if I should trust my gut when it says I'm being blown off. I also have to take into consideration that if this is truly your work that is pulling you away, then I would have to be comfortable going into something knowing that this would continue to happen. I'm not saying that everything has to be about me all the time and that your attention has to always be on me, but I also need to make sure that I continue to value myself and make sure that you do, too. I'm not interested in starting something with someone who sees me as a disposable toy to play with when he wants and then be done with me."

"Wow. Okay. I didn't expect that to be so easy." I shook my head, giving myself a few seconds to process her words before responding.

"I'm sincerely sorry that I had to cancel on you so many times, Paisley. I assure you that it wasn't because I was blowing you off. My cousin injured his back on the job and had to have surgery. I knew that he couldn't afford to take time off for it because he had a wife, three kids, and one on the way to take care of. I stepped in and took the jobs he had lined up so he could work to get back on his feet. I took extra jobs as well to help line their savings so they wouldn't have to worry about things for a few weeks while he recovered. It was never about picking something or someone else over you. But he's my family and needed help, and I was fortunate enough to be in a position to do that for him. I'm sorry that I hurt you in the process, though."

"Thank you. I'm sorry to hear about your cousin."

"He's doing better and recovering well. My other cousin was able to go down there for a few months to help out, which means I won't have to keep going up there for a while. We're a big family, but everyone pitches in when and how they can."

She nodded her head in understanding and cut into her potato. It already felt like the air between us had started to shift with less tension filling the space.

"Thank you for talking to me," I added, cutting a piece of steak and sliding it into my mouth.

"Well, your cock was on the line, and I wasn't about to keep missing out on that."

She chewed with a smug smile on her pretty face while I nearly choked on the bite I had just taken.

# Thirteen

## Paisley

"Do you want anything for dessert?" I asked, looking over my shoulder at Maverick as I washed the forks and steak knives we had used for dinner. "I think I saw some of those individual serving-sized ice cream containers in the frozen food area."

"I absolutely want dessert," he answered, coming up behind me and wrapping his arms around my waist as he kissed the back of my neck. "But it's not ice cream."

"Maverick…." I laughed, squirming as he tickled my sides while possibly leaving a hickey on my shoulder as he kissed and sucked in a way that had me instantly wet. "This is all good and fun, but I really, really want ice cream. You can't deny the heart what it wants."

"I think it's that you can't deny the *cock* what it wants. And this cock wants this warm pussy."

His fingers slipped down over my hips and lifted the hem of the hoodie I was wearing, feathering over my pussy as my ass pushed into his groin.

"What kind of ice cream do you want?" he asked, mercilessly nibbling my ear as his finger slid inside me.

My eyes rolled back in my head as it tilted back to rest on his shoulder.

"Cookies and cock," I answered, not fully paying attention

as he rubbed my clit with his thumb. "Better yet, just the cock."

"I'll go get you ice cream, Paisley. Just tell me what you want."

He acted like he wasn't driving me crazy with his expertly skilled fingers.

I spun around, forcing his fingers out of me as I jumped up, my arms locking behind his neck as my legs wrapped tightly around his waist. My mouth instantly found his, our tongues doing a frenzied dance as the electricity pulsed through us.

My hips began thrusting on their own free will, eliciting a deep groan from the back of his throat. It was harder for me to control myself when I had no panties on and all of the friction was stimulating my clit in the best possible way.

"I don't want to wait anymore," I said breathlessly. "I've waited far too long for you to fuck me, Maverick, so you're going to give me that cock, and you're going to give it to me now."

"Yes, ma'am." He grabbed handfuls of my ass as he lifted me higher and set me on the small countertop.

His mouth found mine as he lifted my hoodie and threw it across the room. Even with the heater working, there was still a chill in the room, instantly hardening my nipples. His hands eagerly reached up and began caressing my breasts, setting my body further ablaze.

My legs spread, inviting him in, though I desperately wanted his cock out.

"You're wearing too many clothes," I muttered between kisses, my hands reaching down to lift his shirt.

"We can fix that." He grabbed the back of his shirt and pulled it off in record time before taking off his sweats. Just like I'd expected, he had been going commando this whole time.

"I don't like to be restricted," he commented, somehow reading my mind.

I reached down and grabbed him, loving how heavy he felt in my hand. I wanted to stroke him and watch ropes of cum squirt across my chest as much as I wanted to take him deep in my throat and feel him release his load. But everything would have to wait until after we fucked this energy out of each other. There was a carnal need, and we were both obsessed with fulfilling it.

He leaned down and pulled a pebbled nipple into his mouth, sucking it to the point I moaned from the pleasure, but borderline painful. I continued to stroke him as I spread my legs wider and lined him up at my entrance. He paused for a second and looked up at me, a million questions flashing across his face.

"I don't have a condom. I get tested every year and am clean. I haven't been with a guy since before I moved to Whiskey Mountain. And I'm on birth control," I said in one long-winded breath. "I just want to feel you without any barriers. Please."

He nodded, his jaw tight as he worked it slowly back and forth as if he was struggling to keep his composure.

"I get tested with my annual physical and got the results back a few weeks ago that I'm clean as well," he confirmed.

I leaned back as much as I could and kept my eyes locked on his as I guided him inside. He was larger than I had expected and I had to pause for a second to allow my body to adjust to his size as he stretched me.

"Shiiitttt," he growled, closing his eyes and gripping my hips tightly to hold me still. "Fuck, Paisley."

"I know," I panted, wrapping my legs tighter around his waist as I pulled him in further. I held my breath as I felt the sharp sting as he slid in deeper, still not fully seated inside me.

"Breathe, baby," he coaxed, gently rubbing his thumb across my cheek. "I know it hurts with how much I'm stretching you, but you can take this cock. I promise. Show me how well you can take it, Paisley."

I nodded my head and closed my eyes, trying to focus on the pleasure part of it as I tried to get my body to relax enough to let him in. He leaned in and nudged my head to the side as he began kissing the side of my neck, my one true weak spot.

My fingers scratched along his back, loving the way he groaned every time I increased the pressure. He lowered his mouth, licking his way down my chest and back to my nipples before pulling one in and sucking hard. This time it was more intense, almost immediately sending me to a mind-blowing orgasm as his fingers found my clit and began rubbing.

"Lean back and rest your head on the cabinet," he instructed, pulling my attention back to him the best I could before he assaulted my other nipple. I did as he asked and felt him grip my waist and pull me closer to the edge of the counter.

His dick was hard inside of me as he rubbed my clit, my legs trembling in response. He wasn't fucking me yet, but he was already bringing me more pleasure than anyone ever had. Within seconds, I felt the tingle up my spine, and then my orgasm washed over me, my pussy violently pulsating against his fingers.

"That's my girl," he said proudly. "Giving me those orgasms when I ask for it. Now you're gonna take this cock and come for me again."

I shook my head, my eyes too heavy to open as he removed his fingers from my clit and held onto my hips again. He began slowly thrusting in and out, each movement deliciously perfect as my pussy adjusted to his size. I was beyond full, loving how deep he was inside of me.

"Are you ready to take this cock, Paisley?"

His thrusts increased as he pulled out and then slammed inside me again before I could even process what was happening.

"Oh my God," I cried, immediately loving the sensation of him thoroughly fucking me.

"I told you that you could take this cock, baby. You're doing such a beautiful job, but I'm not done with you yet. I'm going to fuck you so good you won't be able to walk for days. Which is fine because I plan on eating your pussy while you rest and get your energy back so you can suck my cock like you want to."

His dirty words turned me on so much, and before I knew it, I was on the verge of coming again.

"There it is," he said proudly. "My good girl, already ready to come for me again, aren't you?"

"Yes," I whined, part panting. I shifted myself so I could feel him rub his cock along my clit, the friction and pace precisely what I needed.

"Oh, fuck!" I tried breathing through it, but it was impossible. I grabbed onto him the best I could and closed my eyes as he fucked me hard and rough—exactly how I liked it. The small room echoed the sounds of our bodies slapping against each other, but it was nothing compared to the sweet guttural noise he made as he came inside of me, bringing me to another orgasm.

58

# Fourteen

## Maverick

"Do you want to try the strawberry one?" I offered, extending my spoon to Paisley as we cuddled on the air mattress.

"Sure. Try some of my cookies and cream. It's delicious."

We leaned in and took the bite of ice cream off each other's spoons.

"I like that one, but the strawberry might be my favorite," I said, swallowing my bite before the cold burned my mouth.

"It is quite refreshing. Reminds me of something I would crave on a hot, sunny day."

I nodded, enjoying how relaxed we both were now that we'd fucked all the tension out of our bodies.

"Do you like what you do?" she asked randomly, turning her head to look at me.

My brows pulled together in confusion since there was no context as to what she was asking.

"Like in life? Or as in how I fucked you? Cause if that's what you're asking, yes, I love what I do and can't wait to do it again. I can go now if you're ready." I turned to set my ice cream down as she giggled and grabbed my arm to stop me.

"While I enjoy your honesty, that's not what I was asking."

"Oh."

"I meant, do you enjoy your job? Is heating and cooling what you've always wanted to do?" she clarified.

I shrugged, not really having given it much thought before now.

"I guess so. I don't think I've ever stopped and thought about it. My dad and uncles did it their whole lives, so I was exposed to it at an early age. I enjoyed helping my dad when I was growing up, but I really loved trying to problem-solve why something wasn't working. He always loved watching me struggle to figure it out when he knew what it was within minutes of looking at it. I always hoped I would be as smart as him some day, so it wasn't really a surprise when I went into the same line of work. For others, it can be hard and challenging, but for me, that's what I like the most about it."

"That's awesome. You don't find many people these days who actually love what they do. I always thought Calli was the weird one, but I guess both of you are," she teased, nudging me with her elbow.

"Gee, thanks," I replied sarcastically, nudging her right back. "What about you?"

"Well, I originally moved down here with Calli to help with her mom after her dad died, but there wasn't much more I had planned to do. But now Calli is doing well with the business, and her mom has more support than I could ever give her, so…"

"So…" I prompted, asking her to continue.

"So now I don't know what to do with my life. Everyone else has a purpose, something they love. But not me. I go to work and help Calli, but it's not like she really *needs* me anymore. Do you know what I mean? When we first got Cravings opened, and she was just getting started, yeah, she needed me. Not just for support and to be there as a friend but for help with marketing and drawing in business. Now she has all of that, and the most I do is help at the register or wipe down the tables. I'm easily replaceable now, but not only that, I'm not even doing something that I enjoy. I love going in to work and spending time with Calli, but honestly, she's so busy when we're there that I don't even get to see her as much as I want to."

"If you could do anything in the world, what would you do?" I asked, taking another bite of ice cream.

"Anything—as in there's no monetary restrictions, and I don't have to jump through a million hoops?"

"Yup. Anything. The sky is the limit."

I set my empty ice cream carton down and leaned back against the cabinet the air mattress was pushed up against while I waited for her answer.

"If I could do *anything*, I think I would want to do marketing for a large corporation. I like the idea of being constantly challenged to think of new ideas and see what works."

"Have you looked into any jobs like that here in Whiskey Mountain?"

"No," she said, shaking her head. "I feel bad for even considering doing something different. I agreed to come here to help Calli, so the last thing I want to do is make her feel like I'm abandoning her."

"Yeah, but you said yourself that Calli is doing well, and so is her mom. She is doing what she wants with her life. Isn't it fair that you should be able to as well?"

"I think we all know that life isn't fair, Maverick. I made a commitment to my best friend, and I plan to honor that. But that doesn't mean that I don't sometimes think about what *could* happen if I did something different with my life."

I smiled, but it wasn't one of happiness. I felt sad that she felt like she didn't deserve to live the life she wanted because she was trying to do what she thought was right for her friend. I could get where she was coming from, as someone who always strived to do the right thing and stay loyal to those I loved. But no one had ever asked—or even insinuated—that I put their happiness above my own. It wasn't that Calli was asking her to either, but she also wasn't asking Paisley what she wanted out of life, and that got under my skin deeper than I would have imagined.

"Please don't say anything," Paisley said, turning to face me. "I don't want you to tell Dylan, and then it gets back to Calli. I shouldn't have said anything."

"I won't," I promised, leaning in to kiss her cheek.

But just because I wasn't going to say anything didn't mean I was going to let this drop and not try to find a way to give Paisley the life she wanted.

# Fifteen

## Paisley

I was more tired than expected, probably from having my brains fucked out a few times today—not that I was complaining.

Maverick had been just as good in bed as I had imagined—technically better—but I wasn't going to tell him that and inflate his ego bigger than it already was. Hell, I had already lost track of how many orgasms I'd had today, but I knew if I asked him, he would be able to give me an exact number with a smug smile on his perfectly beautiful face.

We brushed our teeth and climbed into bed, though I wasn't sure you could technically call it that. Sure, it was comfortable for an air mattress, but it was nothing compared to the plush pillowtop one I had waiting for me at home. It hadn't even been a full 48 hours and I was already missing the luxurious conveniences of my house, like having a hot shower and being able to do laundry.

I rolled on my side, facing the wall instead of Maverick, when I felt strong arms grab me and pull me to his chest.

"What are you doing?" I asked with a giggle.

"I thought it was clear when I fucked you earlier that you're mine, but just in case it wasn't, this is me claiming ownership again."

His body pressed against mine, bending and wrapping perfectly against each other.

"I mean it, Paisley," he said when I hadn't responded to him. "Like it or not, you're mine. I licked you. That's the rules of the game: you lick something, and it belongs to you."

"Well, then remind me in the morning to lick your cock, because I'm going to want to take ownership of that if that's what we're doing." I covered my mouth to stifle a yawn as my eyes fluttered closed.

"That's absolutely what we're doing. Goodnight, Paisley. Get some rest."

I tried to say goodnight back to him, but my body was blissfully relaxed, and I was drifting off to sleep within seconds.

When I woke up, I had no idea what time it was—only that my phone wouldn't stop ringing.

I rubbed the sleep from my eyes and tried to open them as I looked around to find it. Maverick's hand extended across my chest, handing it to me as he lay on his back with his eyes closed.

"Thanks," I said, still trying to wake up as I slid my finger across the screen to unlock it. There were two missed calls from Calli, both back-to-back, and I immediately panicked, worried that something had happened to her mom.

"Hey," I said as soon as she answered. "What's wrong?"

"I just saw on the news that there's another storm headed your way. I was waiting for the doctor to come in, and one of those emergency alert things happened. They interrupted the show I was watching to warn everyone about this one."

"Wait—why are you waiting for a doctor? Where are you? Is Mom okay?"

"She's alright. We're at the hospital because she wasn't feeling well. They think it's a cold, but they're going to do a chest x-ray to rule out pneumonia.”

“Oh my gosh, poor thing. Let me know what they say.”

“I will. But the more important question is, how are you? I know it’s only been a few days, but you’re literally living in a general store.”

“It’s surprisingly going alright,” I said, glancing over to see if Maverick was awake. “They have everything we need, so we don’t have to worry about running out of food or water for a while. Maverick got the heater running, so we’re good there. And we’re camping out on an air mattress, so at least we have the basics.”

“Something is off,” she said cautiously.

“No, nothing is off. What are you talking about.”

“Yes, there is. You’re not all angry and spitting venom when you talk about Maver—”

I closed my eyes and waited for her to say it.

“Paisley!” she shrieked loud enough for me to pull the phone away and lower the volume before pressing it to my ear again.

“Shhh,” I hissed, turning my body so I could at least shield myself from having Maverick see the embarrassment flushing across my cheeks.

“You *slept* with him!”

“We’re sharing a sleeping bag so we can stay warmer,” I countered, trying to get up as gently as I could without falling on him. I couldn’t talk to Calli about this sitting right next to him, and I knew she wasn’t going to hang up and *not* demand that we discuss what happened.

I walked down the hall, thankful that we had left the lights on, and then wandered out into the store. It was colder in here, likely due to the large glass windows that seemed to take up the entire wall. Maverick mentioned that he was upgrading the heating and cooling system once the storm passed, which made a lot of sense with how cold it was with the heater running full blast.

"Okay, so by sharing a sleeping bag to stay warmer—did that mean you offered him your vagina so he had a warm place for his dick—because if so, that makes total sense," Calli said. I could just picture the smug smile on her face when she said it.

"Does your mom know you talk like that?" I asked, finding a spot on the counter by the register and hopping up to sit on it.

"We both know that I don't talk to anyone like that except for you. And Dylan," she replied with a giggle.

"Speaking of, how's he doing?"

"He's fine. Stop changing the subject."

I rolled my eyes, hating that she was acting like a total best friend.

"Did you guys sleep together?" she asked.

"Yes."

"Like as in had sex, not just shared a sleeping bag?"

"Yes."

"And was it everything you thought it would be?"

"Yes."

"Okay, so what's the problem? Why aren't you more excited about this?"

"Because it's God knows what time in the morning, and

you called and woke me up. I haven't even had coffee yet," I muttered, looking around to see if they had any fun coffee drinks in the cooler. "You know I'm not a functional human being until I've had some coffee in me."

"I don't know; maybe you should try some Maverick in you and see how *that* starts your day."

"You're so bad." The corners of my lips curled up into a smile as I wondered how that would be. It definitely wouldn't be a bad start to the day…

"The doctor just came in, so I gotta let you go. I just wanted to warn you about that storm. I don't know if anyone can get out to you guys before it hits, but if not, just be prepared that you might be stuck there longer. This one is supposed to be worse than the last."

"Okay, thanks for the heads up. Keep me updated on Mom."

"Will do. Love you."

"Love you too."

I hung up my phone and set it next to me on the counter, wondering if I was truly disappointed that I would be stuck here even longer with Maverick and his wondrous cock.

# Sixteen

## Maverick

"Wow, that snow is really coming down," I commented, looking out the window as it fell in thick blankets around us.

I knew this meant it would be even longer before anyone got to us, but I didn't feel a single ounce of anxiety about being stuck here. It was probably because I had fucked Paisley, so nothing else in the world mattered right now except being in between her legs.

"I don't think I've ever seen snow like this before." She looked past me, her eyes wide as she took in the storm that had officially rolled in. "How long do you think we're going to be here before someone gets to us?"

"Honestly, I don't know. I've never seen it snow this much in such a short time. I don't know if Whiskey Mountian is even equipped to deal with this storm. They have a lot of resources, but at the same time, it's a small city, which means they're still going to be shorthanded, even if they have all hands on deck and get everyone working to clear the roads."

"So, I guess it's safe to say we're stuck here for at least a few weeks after all." She rubbed her hands nervously up and down her arms as her voice rose an octave.

"Hey, it's going to be okay. I promise." I pulled her into my arms and held her, meaning every word I said. "We have everything we need here. Running water. Food. Power. It might not be anything luxurious, but we have what we need to survive being stranded here."

"Okay." She nodded her head, but I could tell she was still freaked out. "I really wish I could just crawl into a hot bath and soak the stress away."

"I think I saw some inflatable kids' pools in the stock room," I offered, a smile teasing my lips as I hoped to lighten the mood.

"I would say that I'll pass on it given that a cold bath sounds terrible—but I also hate the thought of trying to take another shower in the bathroom sink. This place is huge. You would think they would have used some of it for a full-sized bathroom."

I knew by the smile on her face that she was kidding, but something she said sparked something inside that had the wheels in my mind instantly turning.

"Follow me," I said, grabbing her hand and leading her down the aisles as we rushed to the back hallway.

I had been back here a handful of times as I climbed up into the attic to work on stuff, but I'd never opened any of the doors to see what was inside. Before, it was out of respect for Mr. Crawford because I was only here to work on the heating and cooling. But now, who knew how long we would be stuck here, forced to find ways to survive the storm. If I could figure out a way to make that slightly easier, I was going to. I would just have to make it up to Mr. Crawford later.

Paisley followed behind me, not asking a single question as I opened doors and shut them without any explanation of what I was doing. Finally, we reached the end of the hall and I paused, praying that I wasn't wrong about this.

I opened the door slowly and felt the grin spread across my face.

"Bingo."

# Seventeen

## Paisley

I had no idea what Maverick was up to, but when he led me inside the room, I gasped and covered my mouth.

The room was huge, with a massive king-sized bed that looked so much more comfortable than the air mattress we had been sleeping on. Maverick turned on the lights as I walked around, staring in disbelief. There was a nightstand on each side of the bed, bringing an earthy vibe to the room with the dark wood. It was a nice contrast to the light gray and white comforter that covered the bed.

Off to the side was a large walk-in closet that was surprisingly empty. It was big enough that it could probably fit the air mattress we had been sleeping on if we tried. I continued my self-guided tour and turned the corner, walking into the en-suite bathroom and the large soaking tub sitting in the corner.

I continued to stare in disbelief, not quite able to believe all of this was real.

"It looks like that bath is going to happen after all," Maverick said, standing behind me with one hand on my hip.

"I can't believe this. Look at the size of that walk-in shower. We don't have to act like birds and struggle to use that tiny sink in the other bathroom." I turned and faced him, feeling a strange tug on my heart when I did. "How did you know this was back here?"

"Technically, I didn't," he admitted. "When you mentioned it being big enough to have a bathroom, that tickled a memory buried deep in my brain about Mr. Crawford and his wife living here for a bit while their new house was being built. I wasn't sure what, if anything, we would find, but I'm glad we came and checked it out."

"Do you think they'll mind if we use their stuff?"

"I doubt it. The closet and all of the dressers have been emptied," Maverick replied, letting go of me to check the bathroom stuff. "Same in here. Looks like they cleared everything out when they moved into the new house. I can't imagine he would have a problem with us using this space while we're stranded here."

"This feels so unreal," I said, still staring at the giant bathroom in disbelief.

"Want to go get our stuff and bring it in here?" Maverick offered.

"Yes, please. That sounds amazing. I know it's still morning, but I swear, I could climb into that bed and sleep for days. My body already hurts from sleeping on that air mattress."

"Well, how about we go grab our stuff, move it in here, and then you can soak in a long bath. I saw some bath stuff in the store, so there should be a few things to choose from. I also found a washer and dryer in the other closet so we could wash our clothes and pick out some towels. We can even get new bedding if you'd like."

"Why does it feel like we're moving in together?" I joked, meaning for it to sound light and like a joke. But the way Maverick looked at me said he saw nothing funny in it.

***************************

"Oh. My. God." I sank lower into the hot bubbles, closing my eyes and breathing in the calming lavender scent as it floated in the air around me.

"You sound like Janice," Maverick said, standing over me.

Typically, I would be jealous and demand to know who she was, but my body was so relaxed that I didn't have the energy for it.

"Who?"

"From Friends. You know, Chandler's girlfriend?"

"Never seen it."

The water shifted around me as he climbed in behind me. I leaned forward, making sure he had room even though the tub was more than big enough for both of us.

"That's a crime, you know."

"No, a crime is getting out of this tub. It's pure heaven."

"Well, I would agree with that, but I also have fresh, clean towels for you when you're done, and I found new bedding for us and washed it. It's drying as we speak, but a nice, comfy bed will be awaiting you when you're ready."

"Too bad we didn't find a full-sized kitchen," I joked. "I'm not kidding about moving in here just for this tub. This tub is the tub that makes all other tubs jealous."

"I don't think I've ever heard anyone say the word 'tub' that many times in five seconds."

I reached down and pinched his leg, giggling when he tried to pull away.

"Don't talk shit about my tub, or I'll kick you out of it," I warned.

"I think it's technically Mr. Crawford's tub. Or possibly his wife's. I don't know that you can come in and demand that he give it to you."

"I'm going to ask him to rent that bedroom to me. I'll gladly pay him to live there. Plus, it comes with this bathroom and, therefore, the tub. And I wouldn't have to go far to do my grocery shopping. It's like a win/win and dream come true."

"So that's what your dreams are made of?"

"Yup. I've decided what I want to do with my life, and this is it. I can still work at Cravings and live here, enjoying my tub."

While I was technically kidding, I couldn't help but notice how my heart fluttered at the thought of doing something different with my life.

# Eighteen

## Maverick

I got out of the bath a little before Paisley was ready to be done so she could have some space, and so I could get the clean bedding out of the dryer. I was not only relieved to find this room but also ecstatic to find new bedding and a washer and dryer so we didn't have to keep washing our stuff in the tiny sink and hanging it to dry.

The bedroom was more than nice, and the bathroom was an added bonus. I didn't blame Paisley for wanting to live here. I did, too. But that didn't stop my heart from skipping a beat when she jokingly said we were moving in together. If I had my way, I would move in with her in a heartbeat. If she *had* to have this place, I would buy the whole damn place from Mr. Crawford and send him into early retirement while I became the proud new owner of a general store in Whiskey Mountain.

I heard the shower running and knew that she was washing her hair since she didn't want to do it in the bath. The amount of relief that washed over me when we found this space created a sense of peace that I hadn't felt in a long time. It wasn't just about me anymore, but the fact that I was able to keep Paisley as comfortable as possible while being stuck here. While we would have a funny story to later tell our grandkids about us falling in love while stranded in a general store, I couldn't get past the smile on her face, knowing that we had an actual bed to sleep on tonight and that we could do basic things—like taking an actual shower.

A few minutes later, the shower turned off, and Paisley came in with a towel wrapped around her body and one on her head.

"I honestly think I could live here," she teased, pulling the fluffy fabric tighter against her body. "These towels are better than the ones I have at home, which just goes to show that I need to start shopping here instead of the market in town."

"Are you hungry?" I asked, ignoring the lump in my throat as I thought about us living together.

She'd been soaking for a few hours, refilling the tub with hot water when it would go cold. We'd somehow skipped breakfast, which my stomach was currently reminding me of with a loud growl.

"I'm starving. Let me get dressed real quick, and I'll help you fix something if you want."

"Sounds good. Your clothes are in the closet, and your panties are in that drawer," I said, pointing to the large dresser across from the bed with a TV mounted above it. And to think, we spent the first 48 hours stuck in a break room with nothing to entertain ourselves aside from our constant banter.

I left to give her some privacy while she got dressed and went in search of food for lunch. Now that we had the air fryer and power, we had a lot more options. There wasn't much in the way of fresh produce or meat, for that matter. But there was a lot of frozen food that could be easily heated up.

I was scanning the frozen pizza options when Paisley joined me, looking around my arm before grabbing the sausage one.

"Sausage is always the answer," she said, holding it to her chest like some sort of prized possession.

"I'm curious to know what the question is," I teased, picking up a supreme pizza before putting it back and grabbing the pineapple and ham one.

"That's a sin." She pointed to the box in my hand and shook her head.

"You're kidding, right?"

"Nope. Pineapple doesn't belong on pizza."

"I beg to differ."

"You could do the right thing and be Team Sausage. Everyone loves a good sausage."

I grabbed her by the waist and pulled her into me.

"If I were Team Sausage, I wouldn't be giving you mine," I teased, leaning in to nip her earlobe.

"Well, when you put it like that…"

Just before I could nip her again, she pulled away and took off running through the store as I chased behind her. There might have been a storm raging outside, dropping more snow than we could dig our way out of, but there was nowhere in the world I would rather be than here with Paisley.

# Nineteen

## Paisley

"Okay, I'm officially moving in here. I don't care if Mr. Crawford wants to rent this room to me or not. He's either going to take my money and accept it, or he's going to have to find a way to get rid of me because I'm not going easy."

I climbed onto the bed and pulled the comforter and sheet over me, closing my eyes as I inhaled the soft scent of fabric softener. This was so much better than sleeping on the air mattress and being confined to the sleeping bag. The bed was super firm but soft, and the pillow-top mattress added the perfect amount of softness. Not only that, but I had the hottest man in the world in bed beside me, ready to tuck me in or fuck me—either was fine with me.

"I'm glad you like it. Anything would have been better than the air mattress, but this is definitely leveling up a bit." He fluffed the pillow under his head and then laid on his side, facing me.

"I really want you to fuck me senseless on this nice bed we have the privilege of using, but I'm afraid I might fall asleep in the middle of it," I said sleepily, followed by a yawn. "That bath really did me in, and I can barely keep my eyes open."

"No, I would rather you get some rest, Paisley. It's been a rough few days, and we've slept like shit trying to sleep in the other room. Let's get some good sleep and then see what tomorrow brings. It already feels one hundred times better being stuck here now that we found this room. Let's enjoy it, and then we can fuck all day tomorrow.”

“Like a full day fuck-a-thon?” I asked, lifting up on my elbow to see him better.

“If that’s what you want to call it.” He laughed.

“That’s the official name. Now get some sleep and be ready for it.”

He leaned in and lightly kissed my lips.

“Goodnight, Paisley. Sweet dreams.”

“Goodnight. Sweet dreams. Love you.”

My eyes felt heavy as I drifted off to sleep.

***************************************

The next morning, I woke up feeling relaxed, refreshed, and suddenly mortified.

I shot up in bed and stared at the spot where Maverick was supposed to be sleeping. The curtains were still closed so it was hard to tell what time it was, but my guess was that it was too early for him to be up and getting the day started.

I reached over and grabbed my phone, groaning when it showed it was already after eight. I had slept longer and harder than I expected. Last night had felt like such a dream, but I knew for certain that I had said *those words*. I had fallen asleep right away so I had no idea how he’d responded to them, but I was willing to bet money that it wasn’t with *I love you too, Paisley*.

Gah, I was such an idiot. Who confesses they love someone while they’re delirious and sleep-deprived? Not only was it the least romantic way to say it for the first time, it was too freaking early.

We weren’t even dating, and it hadn’t been twenty-four

hours since we'd had sex. I knew Maverick wasn't a commitment or relationship type of guy, so I could only imagine how much this scared him off when I confessed it right after he got in my pants. However, I do blame the lack of pants for what happened between us—not that we needed any excuses.

I climbed out of bed and headed to the bathroom to relieve myself before I burst. A quick glance in the mirror confirmed I looked like the hot mess I was. My hair was tangled and stuck to the side of my face, likely from getting too hot and sweating in my sleep, but also because I went to bed with wet hair. I finished up and washed my hands, quickly brushing my teeth before I had to see Maverick and talk to him about what happened.

It wasn't like I could just ignore it or pretend it didn't happen. There was no way he hadn't heard it, and if I could remember saying it, he definitely remembered as well. The best course of action was to address it head-on and admit that it was a silly slip of the tongue. I was tired, and I'm used to saying goodnight to Calli and her mom, so that's all it was—just a habit of wishing them sweet dreams and telling them I loved them.

But then *why* did it feel so different? If it was really just a tired mistake, why was I so nervous for him to have heard me? I didn't tend to care what people thought about me, but Maverick was different and knowing that what I said must have freaked him out enough to make him get out of bed early was eating away at me in the worst way possible.

By the time I found him, he was pacing in the corner of the store with his phone held against his ear. He was already dressed and wearing new clothes, while his hair looked wet. How had I not heard him in the shower? How long had he been up?

I browsed the refrigerated coffee drinks, pretending to look for a new one to try while he wrapped up his call so I didn't look like the creepy stalker I was. There were three options to choose from, so I grabbed the caramel one and immediately turned it around to read the label on the back as he approached me.

"Good morning," he said, his voice normal and even, revealing nothing about how he felt about what happened last night.

"Oh my gosh!" I said, wayyy too dramatically as I clutched the bottled drink to my chest. "I didn't see you there."

At least the bottle was cold enough to help defuse some of the heat coming off my skin from the embarrassment I was feeling from the lie I'd just told.

"You mean you didn't see me over there taking a phone call when you came out here and watched me for a few minutes before pretending to check out the coffee drinks you've been drinking the past few days?"

"Shit," I muttered under my breath, looking down so he couldn't see my face.

"Look at me, Paisley," he directed, lifting my chin with his finger.

My head lifted, but I looked off to the side to avoid looking at him.

"Nope. Look at *me*."

My heart beat wildly in my chest as I tried to calm myself by counting the types of cheese. I got through Colby Jack, Mozzarella, and Cheddar before he snapped his fingers in front of my face to get my attention again and pulled me out of it.

"What's going on?" he asked, his eyes searching my face for something.

"I don't know what you're talking about."

"Yes, you do. You're being weird and fidgety. Why?"

I blew out a frustrated breath and tried to look away, but he wouldn't let me.

"I don't want to talk about it."

"Well, that's too bad."

"You're quite bossy, don't you think?" I countered with a raised eyebrow.

"No. But I have a *no sex while we're fighting* rule, and I'd like to be balls deep inside you this morning. So the sooner you tell me what's wrong, the sooner I can finally eat your pussy and fuck you again."

My palms started sweating as heat washed over me from his words.

"I said I love you last night when I was falling asleep."

"I know."

"And then it freaked you out, and you weren't in bed when I got up."

"It didn't freak me out. I got up because I had to pee, then I took a shower and when I got out, I had a missed call from Mr. Crawford."

"Mr. Crawford? What did he want?"

"He was calling because he didn't know we were stranded here until he went in for breakfast and Calli told him. I guess he didn't get the voicemail I left him the other day. He wanted to make sure we knew about the bedroom and to tell us to use whatever we needed in the store."

"That was nice of him," I said softly, feeling my heart rate start to come back down a little.

"It was." He held my gaze, not looking away as I started to fidget again.

"You know that I said I love you, and you're acting like it's not a big deal," I blurted out. "Of course I'm going to freak out right now, Maverick. Who wouldn't be?"

"Me."

"Yeah, right," I scoffed.

"I wouldn't be freaked out, Paisley, because I would mean it. I haven't said that I loved you back because I wasn't sure if you meant it or if you said it out of habit. Maybe you say it a lot to Calli or your parents. It's a common thing to say when you're saying goodbye or goodnight."

"Are you saying you love me?" I asked nervously, ignoring everything else he said.

"Yes. I'm saying that I love you, Paisley. I'm head over heels, without a doubt, in love with you. I have been for a while now, but being stuck here together only solidified what I already knew."

"Oh," I whispered, feeling my body flush again, this time with excitement.

"So, what about you? Did you mean it, or were you saying it out of habit?"

I rubbed my lips together, trying to figure out how I really felt. My instinct was to tell him that I loved him too and that I meant it last night when I said it. But I couldn't stop overthinking it and trying to convince myself that I might *not* have said it had I not been so tired.

"Come on, Paisley. Tell me what you're thinking. I've already said it, so you know where I stand. Put me out of my misery one way or another. It's okay if you're not there yet—"

"I love you too, Maverick. I meant what I said last night, and I mean it now. I'm also madly in love with you."

Before I could say anything else, he pulled me flush against his body and kissed me with more passion than I'd ever felt before in my life.

85

# <u>Twenty</u>

## Maverick

It turned out that having a full-day fuck-a-thon was precisely what we needed. My tab with Mr. Crawford was growing by the minute, but we totally needed the extra carbs and hydration to keep up with each other as we kept going at it.

Paisley wasn't just sassy—she was a full-on brat, and I loved every second of it. It wasn't just the way she taunted and teased me; it was the way she trusted me with her body to deliver the pleasure she deserved.

By the time dinner rolled around, I sent her to take a bath while I worked on figuring out what to make. There weren't a ton of options, but I wanted to make something nice for her. I'd taken the time to look up some air fryer recipes and prayed that I could pull them off with a somewhat limited selection of ingredients in the store.

It was nice being stuck here with Paisley, but I hated the idea of what would happen to us once the storm cleared and we were able to get back to our regular lives. We'd said we loved each other, but we hadn't talked about what that meant or what it would look like after we left here. While I would love to move her in with me and spend all of my free time making love to her, I needed to focus on what Paisley wanted.

I knew she wanted to someday work for a large corporation doing marketing, but I didn't know what that meant for us. There were plenty of people in town who worked for large companies remotely, but I didn't want to assume that would be what she would want to do. She was a free spirit, and I could imagine her wanting to travel the world and branch out of this small-town life.

"Something smells good in here," she said, startling me as she came into the breakroom where I was finishing up dinner.

"Thank you. I attempted to make some seasoned chicken breasts with crispy potatoes, but I'm still trying to master this whole air fryer thing." I laughed as I pulled the drawer open and checked on the food.

"Well, I think you're there. It smells better than anything I ever make."

I smiled at her over my shoulder as she took a seat at the table. I had packed up the air mattress and sleeping bag so we could walk easily in here. It was nice having the large closet space in the bedroom to store stuff since I now had a lot to take home.

"Do you want something to drink?" I asked, knowing that the food had at least ten more minutes to cook.

"I'm craving a Diet Dr. Pepper but didn't see any in the drink fridge up front so that probably means I need to stick with water." She laughed lightly, and I loved how much the energy between us had shifted already.

"I'll go see what I can find."

She opened her mouth to object, but I was out the door before I could hear what she said. I scanned the aisles quickly, looking for the section that had the soda. Once I found it, I grabbed a 2 liter and tucked it under my arm while I went in search of a few other things I needed for dinner.

Once I made it back to the breakroom, the food was ready.

I served Paisley first, setting her glass of Diet Dr. Pepper down on the table beside her plate. The way she looked at me with genuine appreciation sent butterflies fluttering through my stomach. I had never felt this way with anyone before, and I couldn't imagine not feeling this way again. Now that I had Paisley, it was my goal to make sure I never let her go.

After we ate, I cleaned up and sent Paisley to the room to pick something to watch on TV. Thankfully, the majority of the storm seemed to have passed, and we hadn't lost power again. I wasn't sure how much signal we would get here, but I had noticed a DVD player set up, and a large selection of movies was stored on the bookshelf beside the dresser. Either way, we would have something to entertain us for a bit tonight.

When I walked into the room, she was cuddled up on the bed, her hair tossed in a loose bun on her head, and she looked incredible. She patted the side of the bed beside her and smiled as she waited for me to join her, but I couldn't stop thinking about how much I wanted this to be our new life.

"What did you pick?" I asked, crawling beside her and inhaling the soft scent of her shampoo from her freshly washed hair.

"There weren't a ton of options to choose from, and most of the DVDs are kinda old," she replied, her nose scrunched. "But I thought this one might be fun. I haven't seen it before."

She held up the case for *What Women Want* and I grinned. It had been a while since I'd seen it, but it was light and funny, while Helen Hunt kinda reminded me of Paisley—a take-charge woman who goes after what she wants.

I shifted and got comfortable while Paisley pressed play to start the movie. It felt like we were on another date, but there weren't any of those first-date jitters to go along with it. We had only been stranded together for a few days, but somehow, it felt like we'd been doing this for years. It felt comfortable, like we were just meant to be together.

# Twenty-One

## Paisley

"That's what I want to do when I grow up," I said wistfully, my attention still fixated on the TV as the movie came to an end and the credits rolled. "I want to be Darcy Maguire, a woman on a mission who goes after what she wants in life. Not letting any chauvinistic weasels like Nick Marshall get in my way or sabotage me."

"Yeah, but he ended up redeeming himself and supporting her in the end," Maverick replied, softly brushing a strand of hair out of my face. "But don't worry, that won't be you."

I pulled my head back in surprise, not sure how to take his words.

"Sorry, I didn't mean that how it came out. You'll definitely be successful in anything you do, Paisley. You're determined, focused, driven. I just meant you won't have to worry about some chauvinistic weasel trying to sabotage you because I'll beat their ass before they have a chance."

The corners of my lips pulled up as my heart swelled at his words.

"Well, lucky for us, we don't have to worry about that anyway—since I won't ever have a highly competitive corporate job. I don't think anyone in Whiskey Mountain is out to sabotage me." I winked to let him know that I was playing, but it seemed to fall short.

"Not yet you don't."

"I hate to break it to you, but I don't think there's ever going to be *that* kind of job here. It's such a small town, I can't imagine they would want to allow a big corporation in like that. Nor could I imagine that a big corporation would want to set up shop in a small town."

"I actually have a friend from college who runs a very successful advertising company in Sugarplum Falls, Idaho. Though he originally started it in New York, he moved to Idaho when his sister passed away and he became the guardian of his niece. While he started in a big city, his branch in a small town is thriving and is actually more profitable than the NY office."

"Wow. I guess I didn't think about it that way. But I think there's a huge difference in success when you already own the company. I don't see anyone doing something like that here."

"No, but that doesn't mean you can't branch out and go somewhere else," he said softly as he felt my body tighten against him.

"You know that's not an option. I can't just up and leave everything here to chase some crazy dream. People might do that in movies, but they don't do it in real life."

"Calli did."

I pulled a deep breath slowly between my lips before letting it out.

"That's different. She came here for her mom. Opening her restaurant was an added bonus."

"Or, maybe it was fate. Maybe she was meant to be here so she could help her mom *and* bring her dream to life."

"You make it sound like it's so easy." I laughed, though I felt nothing was funny about this conversation. He was getting too close to digging up the truth I had been trying to keep from everyone.

"I never said it would be easy. It won't. Change is hard, but so is life. Why go through all of this if you don't have something to live for? Something that brings you so much happiness that you can't wait to wake up the next day to bask in that joy?"

"And what about you? Do you have that?"

"Sometimes." He shrugged. "Maybe not as much with my job anymore, but with you, yeah. If I could wake up every morning to you in my bed, that would be my joy. Having you in my life would be worth waking up every day, getting to love the person who makes my heart whole."

"Then what happens when I find my dream job, and it's not in Whiskey Mountain?" I challenged, holding his gaze as I desperately tried to read the reaction he was hiding from me.

"We would find a way to make things work, Paisley. If you thought I was a pain in the ass trying to get you to talk to me before, then you'll think I'm crazy when you see the lengths I would go to just to keep you in my life."

Butterflies fluttered through my stomach as I tried not to get my hopes up too high. Things right now felt wonderful and perfect, but everything would change once we were forced back into the real world.

# Twenty-Two

## Maverick

I knew Paisley would be mad, but that didn't stop me from reaching out to my friend Jackson this morning to pick his brain about advertising. He had taken Mason, Inc. and built something from the ground up to a multimillion-dollar advertising company all on his own. If anyone could help get me the info on how to get Paisley started, it would be him.

He hadn't answered when I called, which wasn't a surprise, given I knew how busy he would be right now. I left a voice mail, but then not trusting it to go through, shot him a text message letting him know it wasn't urgent but that I wanted to touch base soon if he could.

Paisley was still in the shower while I figured out what to make for breakfast. Even though we had more accommodations than I expected, I was starting to feel frustrated that I didn't have the things I needed. Like a stove. Or more than two dishes. I knew things would change for us as soon as the roads were cleared and we were sent on our merry way, but I was terrified of how much would change for us once we had to figure out what our relationship looked like outside of being stuck together.

I knew she was already feeling frustrated about our conversation last night. She didn't seem to have much interest in looking into a new career path because it felt hard, but I also couldn't just move forward and not want the best for her. Which meant it would be up to me to guide her down that path, whatever it might be.

By the time she finished, I was in the breakroom, plating our food. It wasn't anything fancy, just some potatoes and bacon that I had cooked in the air fryer. Thankfully, it was the pre-cooked kind, so it didn't produce as much grease since I was already worried about it setting the air fryer on fire.

"You didn't have to make me breakfast," she said softly as I set her plate down on the table in front of her. "But thank you."

"It's not what I would have normally made for you, but it's the best I could do with limited resources."

I knew she could hear the agitation in my voice when she reached over and placed her hand on top of mine.

"It's wonderful. Really."

"Sorry," I said with a heavy sigh. "I'm just feeling out of sorts this morning, and I think it's starting to wear on me being stuck here and not having the comfort of being at home. I could have made you a killer breakfast in bed there."

"Yeah? Like what?" She smiled playfully as she picked up a piece of bacon and bit into it.

"I would have made you the most amazing omelet with fresh veggies and the creamiest eggs you've ever tasted. Then I would have made real fried potatoes, the kind my grandma used to make with onions and peppers. I would have cooked bacon and sausage so you could choose what kind of meat you wanted in your mouth—" I stopped and wiggled my eyebrows. "And then I would have topped it all off with a homemade Belgian waffle with fresh whipped cream and berries."

"Sounds like I would have been in a food coma from all of that, but I can't lie—that sounds amazing, and I am super bummed that we're stuck here."

"Me too." I tried to make it sound like I was joking, but I wasn't.

I was used to constantly being on the go, never being in one place for too long. While I enjoyed her company and didn't want that to end, I couldn't help but find myself wishing we had somehow gotten stuck together at my house instead. Not that there was any chance of that actually happening, but it would have been far more comfortable.

"So, what do you want to do today?" I asked, hoping to change my mood.

"Are there options?" Her eyebrows raised in question.

"Not really. Yesterday was a fuck-a-thon, and as much as I would love to do that again, your body needs a break."

She smiled and lowered her eyes bashfully.

"I think I saw a small stack of games. We could always make it a game day," I offered, but I wasn't enthusiastic about it.

"Honestly, I am going stir crazy being cooped up in here and not being able to get fresh air. I know it's only been a few days, but I don't know how people do this. I know it's frigid outside, but I *desperately* want to go out there. Even if for just a few minutes."

"Let's make it happen," I said with a burst of excitement. "It's not like we can't get the front door open. We might not be able to leave and go anywhere, but at least we can get some fresh air."

Paisley smiled as she quickly finished her breakfast. Thankfully, there wasn't much to clean up, so that was a breeze. We changed into warmer clothes, layering with thermal and fleece to keep the cold at bay. I wasn't sure how long we would get to be outside, but even a few minutes would feel like a win right now.

I helped her get snow boots on and then pulled the insulated face mask over her face. She looked adorable, like a cute little snowman that could wobble over at any moment. I pulled mine down and then tightened my gloves, making sure I was ready before attempting to open the door. The wind had died down, but I knew it was going to be blistering cold outside and wasn't sure if it was the best idea to do this after all.

There were a few feet of snow piled against the glass door that led into the store and I wasn't sure I was going to have the strength to push it open. There was a good chance it had froze to the door, and I didn't want to risk breaking the door and then having to deal with finding a way to secure it to keep the heat inside.

I pushed gently, relieved when the snow started to move. It was heavy but thankfully not frozen. I put my full weight against the door, trying not to let Paisley see me struggle as I tried to force it open. Before I could stop her, she was standing beside me, pushing with everything she had.

Finally, we got traction, and a few minutes later, the door opened.

"Holy fuck!" she shrieked, lifting her hands to cover her face as a small gust of wind whipped past us and blew frigid air at us. "It is freezing out here!"

"Maybe this wasn't such a good idea," I muttered loud enough for her to hear.

"It's fine. I'll adjust in a minute. I just didn't expect that."

I guided her as she stepped around the big pile we had created from the door. There was an old wooden bench close by, so I helped her to it and brushed off as much snow as I could so she could sit down. Her teeth were chattering, but I knew she wasn't going to go back inside, even if I asked nicely.

I grabbed the snow shovel from inside and began clearing the mess in front of the door. It felt nice to be moving my body again, even if I was freezing doing it.

Soon, I no longer felt the cold and Paisley seemed to have adjusted to it as well as she sat happily on the bench in her snowsuit. There were more things added to my tab with Mr. Crawford, but I felt better knowing she was as warm and comfortable as she could get, given the circumstances.

I continued clearing the snow, making a pathway from the store to the parking lot. It wasn't like anyone was coming any time soon and would need to use the sidewalk, but it felt good to clear it anyway. I finally reached the parking lot and set the shovel against the wall of the store before heading over to check out the damage to our vehicles from the tree that had fallen.

"How bad is it?" Paisley asked, coming over to join me.

I looked back at her, making sure she was okay before I answered.

"It doesn't look as bad as I thought. Both vehicles are definitely pinned beneath it, but it looks like my truck is taking the brunt of it. If I had a saw, I might be able to cut off enough to free your car."

"You mean like *free* my car, as in we would be able to get in it and leave here?" she asked, desperation in her voice.

"Possibly." I worked my jaw back and forth as my mind ran a mile a minute, trying to figure out how to do this.

"Do you think there are tools inside we can use?"

"I can go check. I don't want to leave you out here by yourself, though."

"Maverick, it's not like I'm going anywhere. Look around; there's nothing for miles. I'll be fine."

I knew she was right, but I still hated the nagging feeling in my gut I had about leaving her.

"Okay, I'll be quick. Stay right there."

"10-4."

Her lips curled into a playful smile, but I missed it as I turned and headed back into the store to see what I could find.

# Twenty-Three

## Paisley

"Oh my God!! I can't believe it!" I squealed, clapping my hands excitedly as I watched Maverick slowly move my car out from beneath the fallen tree. He had been able to cut most of it away, but there was still a tiny bit left that he couldn't get to so he wouldn't allow me to get anywhere near the car while he attempted to move it.

I hated that his truck had been totaled and he would be stuck dealing with the insurance company to get it taken care of, but I was too excited about the idea of going home that I didn't focus on it.

He moved the car to an open section of the lot and parked it before getting out and rushing over to me with a huge grin on his face.

"You did it!" I jumped into his arms, hating how the thick layers of clothes kept us from being as close as I wanted.

"I'm honestly surprised I was able to get it out," he admitted with a grin. "I was even more surprised when it started. Looks like luck is on our side today."

"I can't believe we can actually leave and go home. I can drop you off at your place before I head—"

I stopped speaking when I saw the look on his face.

"Sorry, I just assumed…"

"This is what I was worried about," he admitted, taking a step away from me. "I knew the moment we were able to get out of here, you would take off."

"I'm not taking off," I assured him, reaching for his face when he pulled away. "Maverick, look at me."

His brown eyes refused to meet mine, and that broke my heart.

I lifted my fingers and gently stroked his cheek, hoping he would feel the love I had for him in my touch.

"I'm not taking off," I repeated, stepping to the side so he was forced to look at me. "I'm sorry, I didn't mean to upset you. We haven't talked about what any of this looks like for us once we leave here, and I just figured you would want your space. We've been cooped up together for days, and I wouldn't blame you if you wanted time for yourself."

"No, Paisley. I want time with you. That's all I want."

"Oh. Okay." My heart was racing, and despite how cold it was outside, my palms started sweating.

"But if *you* need time to yourself, that's fine. I'm sorry for acting the way I did. I've just been worried about what would change for us once we weren't stuck here anymore, and I felt like my worst fear was coming true."

"That I would go back to my place?"

He nodded and looked away.

"Don't you think it would be kind of silly of me just to assume that I would go straight to your house? I mean, we've only been dating a few days. It's all kinda moving a little quickly, don't you think?"

I wanted to offer him a way out because there was no way this was what he wanted. How could he? Maverick was adamant about not wanting to be tied down and committed to anyone. He bragged about his lifestyle and how he had the freedom to do what he wanted when he wanted. If I just jumped into this head first, all of that would change.

"I said I love you, Paisley, and I meant it. If I could convince you to move in with me today, I would. And the moment I get a new truck, I'll be at your place, packing your things so you don't have to worry about any of that. So, no, I don't need space. I need you."

I rubbed my lips together, buying myself a few minutes while I considered what he was saying. I didn't have to *move in* with him right now. I could grab a few things and stay with him for a little while to see how that felt. There was no need to rush anything when we were just starting to figure things out.

"Okay, I have a deal," I offered with far too much uncertainty in my voice.

"Let's hear it."

"I'll go to your place and stay for a while, but I don't want to rush moving my stuff over just yet. If we can make it through New Year's without trying to kill each other, I'll officially move in then. That gives us a few months to try this and see where it goes."

"Deal."

He extended his hand for me to shake, but once I took it, he pulled me against his body as his lips crashed down over mine.

"I already told you you're mine, Paisley," he said once we caught our breath. "But if you need a few months to convince yourself that this thing between us is real, so be it."

# Twenty-Four

## Maverick

"This is the master bedroom, and through that door is the ensuite bathroom. I don't know that the tub compares to Mr. Crawford's, but I like to think that it's impressive." I leaned against the doorframe while Paisley looked around, ignoring the feeling inside that told me she was meant to be there.

It took us longer to get home than I had wanted, but between cleaning up our mess at the store and getting Paisley's car loaded with everything we were taking, it was a busy day. I left a note for Mr. Crawford by the register, letting him know that we had left and that I would be back in soon to settle what I owed for the stuff we had used. I left a detailed list of everything, making sure he would find it with the note. I had left him a voicemail as well, just to make sure he was aware that we weren't staying there anymore. It would be a while before I could get back to deal with my truck, but at least we were able to leave and get home.

I expected the drive back to be extended because of the weather, but the trickiest part was making sure it was actually safe enough to drive Paisley's car. There was noticeable damage that she would need to have repaired, but we were both determined enough to get out of there that we figured out a way to make it work. Thankfully, the roads were clear through Whiskey Mountain all the way to Fallen Oaks, where I lived. It wasn't typically a long drive, but we went slower than needed just to be sure the car could handle it.

"This is better than the tub I have at my place, so you won't get any complaints from me." She smiled as she walked in front of it, running her fingers along the sleek edge.

"Well, you're welcome to soak while I figure out something for dinner. The good news is that most of the roads are clear here, so the sky is the limit. I can order food too if you'd rather. Tomorrow, I'll go grocery shopping and can grab whatever you need here."

"You know what I'm craving?" she asked, standing in front of me and batting her eyelashes.

"Chinese food?"

She shook her head, her fingers feathering across my skin as they inched under my shirt and dipped down to my joggers.

"A nice, thick, juicy steak?"

"Nope, but it is thick and juicy."

Before I could stop her, she dropped to her knees, taking my pants down with her.

My eyes rolled to the back of my head as her lips wrapped around my shaft, taking me to the back of her throat.

I had plans of feeding her since we had worked through lunch—but my cock wasn't what I thought would be on the menu. Not that I was complaining.

She hollowed out her cheeks and gripped my ass tightly as she bobbed up and down, her eyes looking up at me from under her dark lashes. I tried to steady my breathing so I didn't come right away, but Paisley was way too good at what she was doing.

"Fuck. I'm going to come, baby," I warned, my hands grabbing the back of her head and holding her steady.

 She maintained her rhythm, not bothering to pull away as I

exploded in her mouth, a sharp breath leaving my parted lips.

Once I was done, Paisley slowly released me and stood up, gently wiping the corners of her mouth as she gave me a devilish grin.

"That wasn't what I was thinking when I mentioned dinner, but if that's what you're in the mood for, I'm more than happy to have my turn eating my favorite thing," I said with wiggled eyebrows.

"While I would love that, my stomach is loudly protesting and wants real food."

"I might have some frozen pizzas in the deep freezer," I offered, not wanting to disappoint her if she wanted something else.

"That sounds perfect. Do you need any help?"

"Nope. I've got it, but thank you. Feel free to look around and make yourself at home. There's plenty of room in the closet for your clothes, and I can go through the dresser soon and clear out some drawers for you. Just let me know what you need, and I'll make it happen."

"I don't want to go all crazy and just take over your house, Maverick." She let out a soft laugh. "I know we agreed to do this for a couple of months to see how it works, but I promise, I'm not coming in to invade your space."

I pulled her against my body and lifted her chin with my finger to force her to look at me.

"I want you to invade my space, Paisley. And I'll keep reminding you of that every single day through New Year's. Then I'll remind you every minute after as I'm packing up your stuff and moving you in with me—permanently. *You* might need the time to adjust to everything and figure out if this is what you want, but I've already made up my mind, and there's nothing in this world that could change it."

# Twenty-Five

## Paisley

"So you're living with him now?" Calli asked as she arranged the creepy little gnomes on the counter by the registers.

"I mean, I guess *yes*, but I haven't *officially* moved any of my stuff in yet. We agreed that we would look at things after the new year and see if everything was still working for us. If he had his way, I would be completely moved in *today*."

"Wow. I honestly didn't expect such a sudden change." She shook her head and kept decorating, but I couldn't help the bitter feeling rising up deep inside at her words.

"What does that mean?"

She looked up at me, then softened her features.

"I didn't mean it in a bad way," she said softly. "It's just that you were adamant about *hating* him a few days ago, and now you guys are suddenly in love and living together. It's a big change in a little time, that's all."

"Trust me, I know." I sat down on the edge of the counter opposite her and sighed heavily. "I've liked Maverick for a while now, and it's not like we haven't gotten to know him here and there. But saying I loved him felt right—which I know sounds crazy."

"It does, but sometimes love happens quickly and you can't stop it. It seems silly to try to fight it if you both already admitted that you're feeling it."

"What if I'm wrong though?"

"What do you mean?" She pulled her brows together as she moved the gnomes again. I hated that I was going to have to see them every day when I came in to work. They gave me the creeps, and I couldn't help but think about the scary movie I watched with Calli a few years ago, where they came to life at night and haunted people.

"What if it's not *love* but maybe just *lust*?"

"As in?"

"As in, I like his cock more than anything else about him. What if I'm so dick-sided by it that I can't see straight, and I think I'm in love, but I'm really just horny or something?"

"Dick-sided?" she questioned with a giggle.

"Yeah, it's like being blindsided, but by a dick."

"I don't think that's a thing…"

"Trust me. It is. If you saw what he was packing, you'd know."

"I'll take your word for it."

She stopped messing with the gnomes and turned to face me. Cravings was already closed for the day and the staff had gone home an hour ago, so thankfully, it was just us.

"I don't think that you're being *dick-sided*. I think you have liked Maverick for a while, but you let your anger and pettiness stand in the way of allowing yourself to get to know him better. Then you got stuck together and were forced to spend all of your time with him for several days, and that helped you guys clear the air. I'm sure that the apparently satisfactory sex helps, but I can tell that there's more to whatever this thing is between you two."

"How?" I threw my hands up, exasperated. "How can you possibly tell that there's more than good sex between us? Because I seriously haven't been able to figure that shit out for the life of me."

"Because you wouldn't be sitting here, freaking out if you didn't genuinely care about him. If it were just sex, you would be forcing me to hear all of the dirty details of the ways he fucked you—even after I beg you to stop. But you're not. In fact, you haven't given me a single detail."

She arched an eyebrow and pinned me with a look that had a rush of heat flushing my cheeks.

"What I'm saying is that you love and respect him enough to treat him as something more than just a good fuck, Paisley. And you're freaking yourself out because you've never been here before."

Why did she have to know me so well?

"So what am I supposed to do now?" I asked, staring at the floor so she couldn't see the look on my face, knowing she was right.

"Enjoy being in a relationship. Put in the effort to make it work. And when you're ready, move your stuff into his house and sell your place. Then get knocked up so I can have a cute little baby to spoil."

My eyes bulged at that last sentence. There was no way I was ready to think about settling down on that level. Living with Maverick—maybe. I could work toward being more comfortable with that. But diving in headfirst and thinking about starting a family right now—no way in hell was that going to happen.

# Twenty-Six

## Maverick

"You're what?" I asked, staring at my dad in disbelief as my jaw hung open.

"I'm retiring. I've reached the age where my body doesn't move like it used to, and I'm too old to be climbing into attics. My knees are getting bad, and my hips constantly hurt. Your old man has worked his ass off for years. It's time I give myself a break and enjoy the life I've created with your mom."

"Wow. Congratulations." My head was still spinning as I tried to process the news. I knew my dad would eventually slow down and consider retiring, but I hadn't expected it to be so soon. He was in good health, but he was getting older, and I would be lying if I said I hadn't noticed he had been slowing down recently when we did a few jobs together.

"Thank you. But the reason I asked you to stop by today is because I wanted to talk to you about the business. I know you've worked hard to get to where you are with your company, but I thought I would see if you were interested in taking over Thompson Mechanical."

My eyes widened as I sat in the chair across from him at the kitchen table, taking it all in.

"But Dad, that's the family company…."

"I know. And you're next in line—if you want it. The business is well established, you know that. I imagine you could easily merge your business with it. The only thing I ask is that you keep the Thompson Mechanical name. People in Whiskey Mountain have known that name for over sixty years. They trust it."

"I don't know what to say." I scrubbed a hand down the scruff of my jaw, shaking my head in disbelief.

While I had assumed this might happen someday, it never occurred to me that it would happen now.

If I took over the family business, that would keep me busier than I was already. I would step into my dad's place and continue running things the way he had and the way my grandfather had before him. My uncles had worked there, too, before they moved away to start their own families. I wanted to make my dad—hell, my whole family—proud.

"The current team would stay in place, so you don't have to worry about any of that. They're good guys and have been with me for years. They know what to do and how to do it. It might be a slight adjustment for some of the older guys since they're so used to me, but they'll be fine."

I nodded, quickly picturing it in my head. I'd dreamed of this since I was a little boy, and now that dream was being offered to me.

 "I'll do it," I said, extending my hand to my dad and shaking his firmly. "I promise I won't let you down."

"I would never offer it to you if I ever thought it was a possibility, son."

He stood up and pulled me with him, wrapping me in a warm embrace as we accepted the new change in the dynamic between us.

*****************************

By the time I finished with work, ran errands, and got home,

I found Paisley in the kitchen making dinner. I set my stuff down on the island and immediately wrapped my arms around her waist from behind as her body swayed to the music coming out of her phone.

"Hello," she said with a giggle as I kissed the side of her neck. "Welcome home."

"Thank you. I'm very happy to be here. Seeing you in my kitchen is the best thing I've seen in a while."

"Is that so?" she asked, turning around slowly as my hands grazed across the silky fabric of the robe she was wearing. She slowly untied it, allowing it to fall to the sides, exposing a matching black lace lingerie set.

"Okay, I lied. Seeing you like *this* is the best thing I've seen in a while."

I reached for her playfully, ready to carry her to my bed and devour her, but she swatted me away.

"Dinner will be ready in a few minutes."

"Okay, but I already know what I want to eat," I teased, growling lowly in her ear.

"You better behave, or I won't give you any dessert." She picked up her spatula and shook it at me.

"Is the dessert you?" I asked, reaching for her again as she turned to face the stove.

"No. I made a pumpkin pie from scratch."

"I'd like to eat your pumpkin pie."

She looked over her shoulder and rolled her eyes, but it did nothing to stop the grin on her beautiful face.

"How was your day?" I asked, not wanting to distract her any more than I already had.

"It was nice. Calli had Dylan come pick me up for work this morning so I didn't have to be ready at two in the morning to catch a ride with her. It'll be nice to have my car fixed so I don't have to keep asking for rides. But it was busy at Cravings, which helped the day go by fast. Calli brought me hom—here, so we got to chat for a little bit on the way."

"I'm glad Calli was able to bring you *home*," I corrected. " I don't mind taking you and picking you up. We can look at our schedules and find something that works."

"I don't want you to be stuck in Whiskey Mountain earlier than you have to be. I can figure something out for now."

"It's not a problem, really. Plus, I'll be spending a whole lot more time there soon enough."

"Oh yeah? Why is that?" She turned off the stove and moved the pan to the trivet, giving me her full attention.

"My dad asked to meet with me today, and during our meeting, he let me know that he's retiring."

"Wow. Were you expecting that?"

"No," I said, shaking my head. "Not at all. I mean, I knew he would eventually, but I guess I just thought he had another ten years or so before he even started considering it."

"So, what does that mean for you? What was the meeting about?"

"My dad wanted to meet with me so he could offer me to take over the company."

Paisley's eyes widened in surprise as her mouth hung open.

"Oh my gosh! Maverick! What did you say?"

I grinned and lowered my head for a second before looking up and locking eyes with her.

"I said yes. I'll officially be the new owner of Thompson Mechanical on January 1st. Until then, I'll still be running my business, but I'll also be making trips to visit the businesses my dad works with in Whiskey Mountain. This way, everyone can get used to the change before it happens. Plus, it allows my dad to get through the holidays and wrap everything up that he needs to before he steps away. It just felt like a new year, a fresh start was the way to go."

"I'm so happy for you. That's incredible news! So does that mean you won't be traveling for work anymore since you'll be taking over the business in Whiskey Mountain?" She wrapped her arms around my neck and hugged me.

"That means I won't be traveling for work anymore. I'll be here permanently. Well, technically in Fallen Oaks, but I could be persuaded to move to Whiskey Mountain…"

"I happen to know of a place," she teased before my lips crashed down on hers.

# Twenty-Seven

## Paisley

The first few weeks of living with Maverick flew by without any issues. It was unsettling how easily we just fell into a routine and how uncomplicated things were. I had expected us to get tired of constantly being in each other's space, but it was never like that.

It was as if he could read what I needed without me having to ask for it. If I was feeling a bit off or grumpy, he would run me a bath and insist that I take some time to relax until I felt better. If I were craving something, he would either cook it or take me out to get it. If I just needed time to myself, he would work on something in a different room or go run errands to give me space.

I liked to think that I was doing the same for him, but I found early on that Maverick was never one to ask for anything or complain. He always had a smile on his face, and whenever I asked him if there was anything I could do for him, he would find a way to twist it around to see what *he* could do for *me*.

Thanksgiving had come and gone without the threat of another massive snowstorm they had predicted—which was nice. Thankfully, it wouldn't be bad if we got stuck together again since this time we would have the comfort of his house, but we also weren't stranded in the middle of nowhere waiting for someone to come rescue us.

We celebrated at Calli's house, where she cooked an elaborate meal. It was nice to see some of our friends, but

I was more interested in checking on her mom to make sure she was doing okay. I'd spent so much of my time helping Calli care for her when we first moved to Whiskey Mountain that it felt weird not to be as involved anymore. Not only that, but her mom stepped in and raised me after I lost mine when I was little, so it felt a little like I wasn't being there for her like a daughter should.

Even though I was happy living with Maverick, I couldn't shake the feeling that something big was going to happen. A change neither of us would see coming.

"So, did you decide what you're going to get him?" Calli asked, nudging me with her elbow as I wiped down the counter. Our morning rush was over, but I was already too tired to face the lunch crowd that would be coming in soon.

"Get who what?"

I frowned as I tried to stifle a yawn. I hadn't slept well last night with the wind howling, keeping me awake.

"I was asking if you decided what to get Maverick for Christmas. It's only two weeks away, Paisley. You're going to run out of time."

"I haven't." I sighed heavily, jumping up to sit on the countertop, even though I knew she hated it when I did that. "I have everyone else done except him."

"Do you want me to ask Dylan and see if he has any ideas?"

"No, but thank you. I already feel like shit for not knowing what to get my boyfriend for Christmas. I would feel worse if I had to sink to asking his friend what to get him. I mean, I live with the guy. I should know what he wants."

"It's hard picking gifts for a partner when you're in a new relationship. I struggled with what to get Dylan." She shrugged as if we were in the same boat.

"Are you kidding me?" I tipped my head back and laughed. "Calli, you have at least twenty gifts for him under the tree. I think your problem was knowing when to stop," I teased.

"Maybe. But I'm a good gift giver. It just comes easily to me."

"Okay, then tell me what to get the guy who has everything and wants nothing. That can be your gift to me this year."

"I don't think so. I already got your gifts, and you're going to love them."

I pouted my bottom lip and made it quiver, hoping she would take pity on me.

"I don't know Maverick as well as you do, but from what I know about him, I would go along the lines of apparel. He's more than just a basic t-shirt and jeans guy, so maybe a nice button-down shirt or a scarf that would go with the leather jacket he loves wearing? Or maybe some new gloves? You could also get him some of the cologne he wears. He always smells so good."

"Why are you smelling my boyfriend?" I asked playfully, giving her a look as her cheeks flushed with embarrassment.

"I'm not! I mean, it's not like I'm going up to him and straight up sniffing him. I just notice it because it lingers in the air around him."

"Relax, I'm just teasing."

"Don't tell Dylan I said that his friend smells good. I'll never hear the end of it."

"Maybe you should get him a bottle of the same cologne since you like it so much. You can go around smelling your own man."

"I did. It's not the same."

My eyes bulged as I tried not to burst into laughter.

"What?" I snorted, lifting my hands to my mouth.

"I bought him the same cologne, but it doesn't smell the same on him as it does on Maverick. Don't you dare tell him that, though. I'll cut you…"

"Your secret is safe with me." I held my hands up in front of me.

"Thanks. But honestly, I think he's going to love whatever you get him. You could wrap a bow around yourself, and he would love it."

I knew she was just being sarcastic, but suddenly, I had an idea.

"You're a genius!" I hopped off the counter and grabbed my phone before heading to her office. I didn't need anyone looking over my shoulder or seeing what I was about to look up.

# Twenty-Eight

## Maverick

"Do you know her size?" the woman behind the glass counter asked as I held up a beautiful diamond ring and examined it.

"Unfortunately, I don't. I can find out, though."

"I think it's so romantic that you're going to propose on Christmas morning. It's not often that we get to hear the story of how someone is planning to do it."

"Can I be honest?" I asked, peering up at her. "I didn't know I was going to do this until about twenty minutes ago when I was walking past your shop to get to Spill The Beans. Something just clicked, and I knew I wanted to do this. You're the only one who knows about it, so I trust you won't say anything to anyone in town. We know how quickly news like this can travel in a small town…"

"Oh, of course. My lips are sealed. I won't say a word. And the good news is it's less than two weeks until Christmas, so you won't have to keep the secret too much longer. But I do worry about not knowing what size ring you'll need. If we don't have that size in stock, I would have to order it, and that would take—"

She stopped talking as I lifted my finger to stop her and held the phone to my ear.

"Cravings, how can I help you?"

"You're just the person I was looking for," I replied, pressing the phone closer to my ear to keep the saleswoman from overhearing my conversation. "I was hoping to ask you something without Paisley hearing."

"Sure, what's up?"

"Is there any way you can find out what size ring she wears?" I felt my jaw tighten as I asked, knowing that Calli would absolutely know that I was shopping for an engagement ring.

"Six."

"Six?"

"Yes, we will close at *six* on Friday, so if you'd like to come pick up your order for your dinner party, I'll be here to give it to you."

I frowned, wondering if she had missed what I was asking for.

"Sorry, she came up front, so I had to make something up," Calli said quickly, her voice drastically lower than a few minutes ago. "She wears a size six ring and prefers rose gold, however, if that's not an option, she'll love whatever you pick. Nothing big, gaudy, or flashy. She likes simple and dainty."

"Thanks, Calli."

"Anytime."

I was grinning like a fool as I hung up the phone and let out a heavy breath.

"Do you, by chance, have that in a size six?"

"It's your lucky day," the saleswoman said, her smile now matching mine. "There's one left."

After I finished up at the jewelry store, I rushed over to Spill The Beans for a latte before they closed. I was supposed to be meeting with clients today with my dad, but he was feeling under the weather so we rescheduled. Since my calendar was already cleared on my side, I decided to take the day to finish my holiday shopping since I had been struggling with what to get Paisley.

I knew her well enough by now to know what she would like, but every time I considered getting something, it felt like it wasn't good enough. I wanted her to know how much I loved her and needed her in my life, yet I couldn't find the perfect thing to convey that until now.

With the ring secure, I headed through the strip mall, finding a few other small gifts that I thought she would like.

By the time I was done, I was too tired to go home and cook, so I sent her a text message to see if she wanted to stay in town for dinner.

**Me: Hey baby, do you want to do dinner in town?**

**Paisley: That's so funny; Calli literally just asked if we wanted to go to La Salsa with them tonight as your text came through.**

**Me: Sounds like fate.**

**Paisley: We don't have to go with them if you had something else in mind.**

**Me: Not at all. I'm just tired and didn't feel like going home to cook. We can go with them if that sounds good to you.**

**Paisley: I could totally get down with some tacos and queso tonight. Maybe a margarita since I got to be a passenger princess today.**

**Me: You can have five margaritas if you want.**

Paisley: Is that because of that song?

Me: ???

Me: What song?

Paisley: You know, the one that's all over social media where she talks about the stuff she'll do based on how many margaritas she's had.

Me: I haven't heard it, but I might look it up now… you know, just for reference.

Paisley: Trust me, you don't need me to be filled with margaritas. You can have whatever you want.

Me: Well, in that case, maybe we should skip dinner and eat at home instead. Or in my truck. It doesn't matter where we are—I'll eat you anywhere.

Paisley: As tempting as that sounds, my heart—and stomach are settled on tacos.

Me: Fine, you can eat your tacos now, and I'll eat mine later.

Me: Do you want me to come pick you up, or are you going to ride over with Calli?

Paisley: I can ride over with her. Where are you at?

Me: I was finishing some shopping, so I'm actually right across the street from La Salsa.

Paisley: Perfect! We're wrapping up now and can head over if you want to go grab us a booth in the back.

Me: I'll see you soon.

Paisley: Love you.

Me: Love you more.

I tucked my phone back into my pocket and headed over to the restaurant.

It was busier than I had expected, especially for the middle of the week. But then again, it was close to all of the major stores in town, and everyone seemed to be rushing to get their shopping done.

By the time the girls got there, Dylan and I were already holding the booth everyone liked, and food had been ordered since we knew what they wanted. It was nice to feel as in sync with Paisley as Dylan was with Calli.

"I'm gonna run to the restroom real quick," Paisley said, getting up from the table and rushing off.

Once she was gone, Calli leaned in and locked eyes with me as she kept her voice low.

"Did you get it?"

I nodded, glancing briefly at Dylan to see if he had any idea what was going on. I looked around to make sure Paisley was still in the bathroom before pulling the ring out of my inside coat pocket and passing the box to Calli.

She looked over her shoulder to make sure it was clear before opening the box. A soft gasp escaped her lips as her eyes teared up. She leaned in to show Dylan, who smiled warmly at me before wrapping an arm around her shoulders.

"Oh my God, Maverick. She's going to love it. It's perfect." She quickly closed the box and passed it back to me before Paisley came back.

"Thank you. The moment I saw it, I knew it was the one."

"When are you going to do it?" Dylan asked.

"Christmas," I rushed out, shoving it back into my pocket as I spotted Paisley heading our way.

"I told him it would have to wait until next year for a job that big," I said a little too loudly, drawing the attention of those at nearby tables and earning a confused look from Calli and Dylan in the process.

"What did I miss?" Paisley asked, sitting down and looking around the table.

"Oh, nothing. I was just telling them that I had to push back a big project until next year. Things are just too busy right now with merging my dad's business and mine."

Before she could question anything, a scrawny kid came over with our food.

I sighed heavily, thankful for the distraction. There was nothing I wanted more than to marry Paisley and spend the rest of my life with her—but I was going to be a nervous wreck trying to keep this secret from her until Christmas.

# Twenty-Nine

## Paisley

"Are you sure about this?" I asked, suddenly doubting myself as I ran a hand across the thin fabric that was attempting to hide my stomach.

"Yes!! Now get your ass out here and show me how hot you look," Calli called, making sure I could hear her through the bathroom door I was hiding behind.

I had the wild idea to do sexy Christmas-themed boudoir photos for Maverick for Christmas but hadn't taken into consideration the time I would need to pull all of this together. Thankfully, Calli was entirely on board and agreed to not only take the photos for me but also had a great printer so we didn't have to have that awkward conversation trying to get them printed in town.

I took a deep breath in through my nose and released it slowly through my mouth, trying to calm my nerves. There was nothing to be this nervous about, yet it was like I was getting ready to walk down Main Street, strutting my stuff for everyone to see.

"I know we have the room for the entire day, but we're going to lose daylight if we don't get started soon."

"Okay, okay," I replied, opening the door. "I'm coming."

I walked into the room, thankful that we had gotten one on the top floor so no one could see in the windows that were completely open, letting in enough natural light to not need any other lights on.

"Holy. Shit."

Calli's jaw dropped open as her eyes widened and a smile started spreading across her face.

"You look amazing!"

"Thanks," I said nervously, still rubbing a hand across my stomach. "I was going for a naughty Mrs. Claus look."

"Umm, I think you nailed it."

I stepped in front of the floor-length mirror, taking in the red bodysuit I was wearing and the white fur that lined the long sleeves, the deep plunging neckline, and the bottom of the skirt that barely covered my ass. It was a corset style that laced up the front, putting my breasts on full display with just a hint of skin that showed between the laces. I wore the red thong that came with it, but for the most part, it was covered by the skirt.

I adjusted the Santa hat on my head, then pulled on the knee-high black stiletto boots I had brought to go with it.

"He's going to love this," Calli said, checking the settings on her camera as I applied red lipstick to finish the look.

"I really hope so."

Calli gave me a look that said I was being ridiculous, then guided me to where she wanted me. We did a handful of photos with me standing in front of the window or sitting on the tiny ledge as I spread my legs seductively. Part of me wondered if anyone could see me, and I couldn't deny the heat that was spreading through me at the thought that maybe they could.

I climbed onto the bed and got into the poses she asked for, along with a few of my own that just felt natural. It was better to have too many photos and not be able to use all of them than to not have enough. This was his main gift from me for our first Christmas together, and I didn't want to screw it up.

We spent a few hours doing photos with some wardrobe changes in between. Calli loved the Mrs. Claus outfit, but I found myself torn between the naughty elf get-up and the snow bunny one. It was more fun than I imagined it would be, especially after my nerves settled.

"Okay, this is the last one, and then we can stop and grab dinner," I said, coming out of the bathroom in a black leather lingerie set that was giving some serious dominatrix vibes. I knew this would probably be Maverick's favorite and wanted to make sure I did it right with some more risqué photos.

I climbed onto the bed and got onto my knees, making sure not to damage the white comforter with my heels as I spread my legs. My hair was pulled up into a high ponytail for this one, and my makeup darker with a dramatic smokey eye look. I felt more confident like this than I had in any of the other photos. I moved freely, getting into the positions I wanted as Calli snapped the photos, telling me how much she loved all of them.

Before we finished, I decided to do one last pose—just to be cheeky. I got down on all fours on the bed and angled myself so she could get the picture from behind. I knew Maverick loved my ass and that this picture would drive him crazy. To up the ante, I spread my legs, looked over my shoulder, and lowered my hand so my fingers were pushing the thin fabric of my thong to the side. My lips were exposed, but I knew I wanted to go all in with this, so I slowly slid one finger inside, knowing Calli wouldn't be bothered by any of it. Heck, I had helped her do something similar for Dylan a while back.

"He's going to go crazy over these," Calli said, getting the last picture so I could pull my hand away and fix my panties. "Let me get one more from the side."

She bent to take the picture, but I noticed an odd frown on her face as she looked at me through the viewfinder.

"What's wrong?" I asked, wondering if something had happened to the lingerie or if I had accidentally popped a titty out or something.

"Nothing," she rushed out, lowering the camera quickly. The look on her face confirmed she was lying.

"What is it?" I probed, suddenly feeling super self-conscious.

"It's nothing. I promise."

"Stop lying to me, Calli. You're my best friend, so act like it."

She rubbed her lips together and avoided looking at me as I climbed off the bed and stood in front of her. I raised my eyebrow, forcing the question again.

"I noticed a small bump and my mind just immediately got ahead of me before I could process what I was thinking."

"Small bump? Where?" I rushed over to the mirror, wondering what sort of skin abnormality she had seen that I wasn't aware of. Was it a pimple? Ingrown hair? A wart? Now my mind was spiraling out of control, wondering what she had seen that had freaked her out.

 "Calli, where is it?" I asked, panic thick in my voice. "Where's the bump?" I turned quickly, my eyes scanning every inch of my body in the mirror as I desperately tried to find what she had seen.

"Here," she said softly, rubbing her hand over my lower stomach.

Her eyes lifted to mine in the mirror and it was at that moment that I knew.

# Thirty

## Paisley

"When was your last period?" Calli asked as we sat on the hotel bed, unwrapping the boxes of pregnancy tests she had run out to purchase.

"I don't know." My mind was racing a mile a minute, and all I could focus on right now was getting the stupid test sticks out of their packaging. Why was it so hard? Didn't they know most women would need to get to these in a hurry?

"Paisley, calm down. We don't even know if you're pregnant. I shouldn't have said anything. I just saw it, and I don't know… I guess I just thought maybe…"

"No, I'm glad you did. God knows I probably wouldn't even know until nine months later when I was having a kid on the toilet or something."

She reached over and grabbed my hands, stopping me from the panic attack I was about to have.

"Let's not freak out until we know for sure, okay?"

I nodded my head and took in a shaky breath. Maverick had checked in earlier to see how things were going, but he knew I was staying with Calli tonight, so he told me he would give us some time to ourselves. I was kinda thankful that I didn't have to worry about talking to him right now. We didn't need everyone freaking out until we knew for sure what was happening.

I got up and went into the bathroom to pee in one of the disposable cups we found in the room. I pulled the plastic off of it, sat down, and closed my eyes while I tried to get it together.

"You ready?" Calli asked from the room as I stared in the mirror after washing my hands.

"Yeah. Let's get this over with."

She joined me at the vanity and gave me a reassuring smile as she handed me a few sticks that had been removed from the packaging. We each took turns dipping them into the cup, then put the caps on and laid them on the plastic bag from the store. In three to five minutes, I would have answers and would know whether my life was about to change forever.

"We can sit down while we wait," she offered, gently leading me back to the bed.

"How long has it been since you guys got stuck together in that storm?"

"I don't know," I said with a heavy sigh, trying to remember. "That was at the beginning of November, I think? I was there to get those stupid gnomes for you so you could decorate for Thanksgiving."

"That's right. Okay. Let me check my calendar real quick."

I waited while she scrolled through her phone, doing some sort of period math in her head.

"And you don't remember the last time you had your period?"

I shook my head and tried to force my shoulders down from my ears.

"Okay, so that was about seven or eight weeks ago. And you guys did it while you were there, right?"

I nodded, trying to remember the details.

"Yeah, we spent one whole day doing it. It was a fuck-a-thon," I said with an awkward laugh while I chewed my nail.

"Okay, then," she replied with a little giggle. "I don't think we're going to have any questions about *how* this happened if those tests are positive. Did you guys use protection?"

"No."

"At all?"

"I'm on the pill," I said with a shrug. "It's supposed to work."

"Yeah, but Paisley, birth control pills are only like 99% effective. Did you have them with you while you were stranded?"

"Nope," I said, quickly realizing where this was going. "I missed a few days while we were stuck there."

"And then you moved in with him and have been fucking nonstop ever since?" she asked with a smirk.

"Yup."

"Well, then, I guess there's only one thing left to do."

"What's that?"

"Let's go check the test and see if you're knocked up."

She got up and extended her hand, but I refused to take it. I looked up at her, tears welling in my eyes as I shook my head.

"I can't do it. Can you please tell me?"

"Okay." She nodded her head, squeezed my hand, and then walked back to the bathroom.

I had no idea how long she was really gone because minutes felt like hours as my lungs burned trying to pull air through them.

"Calli, you're killing me," I whined, wringing my hands together nervously.

She came around the corner holding three tests in one hand while covering her mouth with the other.

I opened my mouth to speak, but the words refused to come out.

"Congratulations, you're gonna be a momma," she said, her voice breaking with emotion at the end.

***********************************

"Are you sure we shouldn't order real food?" Calli asked, staring at my second bowl of banana split that we'd gotten with room service.

"No. I'm apparently eating for two, so that justifies having two bowls of ice cream," I countered, my nerves still shot.

"Yes, but I worry that you're going to crash soon from all of this sugar, and I'd like to have some protein ready before they close room service for the night. I don't want to have to call Dylan and have him bring us food, especially with you in this state," she teased, pointing to the chocolate syrup smeared across my cheek.

"I'm fine. Really. I mean, who wouldn't be? I just started dating someone who I got stuck with in a general store during the most bizarre blizzard in the history of blizzards, only to have my birth control fail and get knocked up. Not only that—but I'm getting fat early, so why not justify it with some freaking ice cream?" My voice was so high-pitched that it even scared me.

"Okay, I'm just gonna make a quick phone call," she said

warily, grabbing her phone and stepping into the hallway.

"You better not be calling Mav—" I started before the sound of the door closing cut me off.

I knew I needed to tell him I was pregnant, but I wanted some time to process the news myself before I ran off and scared him, too. If she could spot a baby bump on me this early, it would be impossible for him to miss it. However, a quick Google search confirmed that I likely wasn't actually showing yet and that it was probably slight bloating—not that I was helping anything by eating all of this ice cream.

A few minutes later, Calli came back inside and sat on the bed as if nothing had happened. She grabbed the remote and started flipping through the channels on the TV without saying anything about who she had called or what was happening. I knew her well enough to know without a doubt that something was up.

"Are you seriously not going to tell me what you did?" I asked, finishing the last of the ice cream before setting the empty bowl on the nightstand between us.

"Nope."

"Why?"

"Because it's better that you don't know. You're already all twitchy as it is."

I frowned and stared at the side of her head, willing her to look at me.

"Stop it. I'm not going to tell you anything. But I do suggest you go wash your face. You still have chocolate on your chin."

I stuck my tongue out at her before getting up and relieving myself again before washing my face. By the time I got back to the bed, she was sitting there with her head down, focused on her phone.

"It should be here in a few minutes."

"What should?"

"Your care package."

I sat on the bed and took a deep breath, loving that I had someone here to help me through this right now. Not that I didn't have Maverick, but I wasn't in any condition to tell him right now. Not when I was still a mess and unable to wrap my head around how I felt.

A few minutes later, there was a soft knock on the door. Calli got up and opened it, my body immediately going into panic mode when I heard Dylan's voice. I wasn't sure if she had told him to bring Maverick with him and that was supposed to be my care package.

I couldn't hear what they were saying and sat rigidly on the edge of the bed as they talked quietly in the hallway. I was getting ready to get up and pace the room when I heard the door shut, and Calli walked toward me with two bags in her hands.

"Real food because you need it," she explained, waving the bag of takeout from La Salsa. "And a self-care package because you need it. But because we're doing self-care, I say we start with food because that's a priority right now. Plus, you don't let good tacos go bad."

I laughed and felt some of the tension release from my shoulders as I joined Calli at the small table in the corner of the room by the window. She unpacked the food and pulled out a few bottles of water that she set between us.

She passed a to-go box of chicken tacos my way, knowing my order perfectly. I grabbed a chip from the box in between us and dipped it into the salsa, closing my eyes as my stomach growled loudly. Calli laughed as she took her food out and set the bag on the floor behind her.

"Thank you for ordering dinner. Sorry I was being so difficult."

"It's not a problem at all. I'm just thankful you're eating something other than ice cream," she joked.

"Yeah, I might have to change my eating habits if I don't want to gain a bunch with this preg—"

The words died in my throat before I could get them out.

"It's all about balance. You can indulge in the sweet stuff, but just make sure you're eating plenty of healthy stuff, too—and lots of water. You'll want to make sure you limit how much caffeine you're drinking as well," she said before taking a bite of her food.

"You know so much about this," I commented without thinking. "I have no idea what I'm doing, and you seem to be a wealth of knowledge."

"I had Dylan stop and grab some stuff for you while he was out getting dinner," she said, ignoring my comment. "You'll want to start prenatal vitamins right away. I had him grab these ones since I like them."

She reached down, grabbed a bottle from the other bag, and passed it to me.

"Oh, thank you. That's so sweet of—"

I stopped and narrowed my eyes at her as she suddenly looked away from me.

"Calli?"

Slowly, she looked up at me, her eyes quickly giving her away.

"What do you mean these are the ones you like?"

She rubbed her lips together as she leaned back in the chair and thought about how to respond.

"The pill ones are hard to swallow for me and have a bad smell that makes me more nauseous. I like the gummy ones better and thought you might too."

I leaned forward and looked her in the eyes.

"Calli, you're pregnant?"

She nodded, lifting her hands to brush away the tears.

"Oh my God! Why didn't you say anything?"

I jumped up from my seat and pulled her up to hug her. I wrapped my arms around her, squeezing every emotion out of us, before stepping back and looking at her stomach.

"I just found out a few weeks ago. We were waiting until after our first doctor's appointment before telling anyone."

"I can't believe this. So we're going to be pregnant together?"

She nodded her head, tears sliding down her face.

"When is your appointment?"

"Next week. It's the day I have myself leaving early."

"Wow. This is so wild. Do you know how far along you are?"

"Not exactly, *but* I think I'm around ten or eleven weeks."

"How does Dylan feel about it?"

"He's already in love and keeps saying it's a girl," she said with a laugh. "I think me being pregnant is what led me to thinking you might be when I saw your little bump. Dylan is constantly checking to see if he can see one on me, so now I'm obsessively looking for it."

"That's so awesome. I'm so happy for you guys!" I gave her another squeeze before letting her go so we could finish our dinner. "He's going to be such a great dad."

"Maverick will be too," she said softly. "And I already know he's going to be just as excited as Dylan was when he found out. We won't say anything about you being pregnant until you tell him yourself. Just be sure to do it soon. You don't want him to miss out on being there for you, Paisley."

I nodded and popped a chip into my mouth, giving it some thought.

"I guess I ended up finding the perfect Christmas gift for him after all," I replied with a laugh. "I mean, that is if I can go five more days without telling him."

# Thirty-One

## Maverick

It had been the longest two weeks trying to keep the proposal from Paisley. I kept almost slipping up, calling her my wife and then having to play it off as some weird thing that couples that lived together did. She seemed distracted the past few days and didn't seem to pay it as much attention as the first few times I'd done it, but then again, she might have just gotten used to it. Or maybe it wasn't as easy to freak her out anymore after all.

I rolled over and pulled her close to me, inhaling the soft scent of her shampoo as she turned and faced me.

"Good morning," I greeted, giving her a few minutes to wake up.

"Good morning."

Her eyes were still closed but she looked more beautiful than ever.

"Merry Christmas."

"Merry Christmas," she replied as her eyes slowly fluttered open.

I didn't want to rush her, especially since we didn't have anything pressing to do until dinner this evening at Calli and Dylan's house. But I was so anxious to finally get to ask her to marry me that I felt like a kid standing in front of a candy shop, begging my parents for an early allowance.

"I know it's early," I said as calmly as I could. "But I want to give you your present."

"Okay, go for it," she said sleepily, her eyes fluttering closed again as she shifted and spread her legs. "I'll enjoy it. Promise."

"As romantic and tempting as that sounds, eating you out is not my gift to you. I have something that I *hope* you'll enjoy even more."

"Okay, okay. I'll get up. I have something I want to give you, too."

She seemed more tired than usual, which made me feel bad for pushing her to get up.

"How about I go make us some breakfast before we open anything? You can take your time getting up and around while I start a pot of coffee."

"No coffee for me. I'm not supposed to have caffeine."

I pulled my head back in confusion as she slowly climbed out of bed before suddenly stopping. It was as if she realized the words she said as she said them, frozen in place as her face turned white as a sheet.

"Why aren't you supposed to have caffeine?" I questioned, stepping closer to her.

She opened her mouth and then snapped it shut, clearly not ready to say whatever was trying to come out.

"Paisley…"

I didn't want to push her, but my mind was already racing with reasons why she couldn't have it.

"I umm. Well…"

"You're killing me here."

I stepped around the bed and stood in front of her, grabbing her hands and holding them in front of me.

"Paisley, what's going on?"

"I'm pregnant."

My body temperature spiked as my heart started racing with excitement.

"You're pregnant?" I asked in disbelief.

She nodded, her eyes clouded with tears as she tried to look away.

"Baby, what's wrong?"

I pulled her into me and wrapped her in a protective embrace.

"Nothing, I just do this now. I cry over everything," she sobbed, digging her head into my chest.

"Are you okay?"

"Yeah, just a little nervous to tell you. I had planned to do something for you as a gift to tell you the news, but I ran out of time."

"Paisley, you being pregnant is the best gift you could have ever given me."

My eyes traveled down her body to her stomach, where I placed my hand.

"Are you really okay with this?"

"Of course. Why wouldn't I be?"

"I don't know, Maverick." She sighed heavily, sitting on the edge of the bed and looking up at me. "We didn't plan any of this. We weren't trying to have a baby. All of this kind of just fell into our laps, and bam—now I'm knocked up with your child."

"True, we didn't plan any of this, but I also wouldn't have it any other way." I reached down and lifted her chin to look at me again as she tried to look away. "I told you that I want a life with you, Paisley. This has never been something temporary for me. I've wanted you from the start, and I wasn't kidding when I told you that you were mine. Having a baby with you just strengthens the connection between us."

"Yeah, but we just started living together. Don't you feel like all of this is kind of rushed? I mean, call me crazy, but I thought I would be married and stuff before I started popping out babies."

I arched an eyebrow, wondering if she knew about me proposing.

"I mean—I wasn't saying you need to marry me because I'm carrying your child. That's not what I meant. I just always thought that *if* I had kids with someone, we would be—"

"Paisley," I said, interrupting her.

Her face was the cutest shade of red as she tried to avoid looking at me.

"This isn't how I was planning to do this," I muttered, walking over to the dresser and grabbing the ring box. "But if the time is right…"

I stood in front of her and smiled before dropping to one knee and opening the box to face her.

"I had this really romantic proposal planned," I explained with a laugh, shaking my head. "I was going to do it in front of the tree with the beautiful snowy background behind us. I even had a camera set up so I could get a picture of it."

"Oh my God!" she squealed, covering her eyes and dropping her head. "I'm ruining everything this morning!"

I reached over and grabbed her hands, forcing them down.

"You're not ruining anything. Just because this isn't going according to how I thought it would doesn't mean this isn't the perfect way to propose."

"You're just saying that to make me feel better."

"I'm not. But I do have something to ask you."

She took a deep breath and slowly released it as she looked down at the ring in my hand.

"Paisley, I love you more than I have ever loved anything. Being with you makes me feel like my life is complete, and I cannot imagine spending another day without you beside me. Would you do me the honor of marrying me and being my wife?"

Her bottom lip quivered as she looked from me to the ring and then back to me.

"Yes," she said, her voice shaky as she reached forward and wrapped her arms around my neck.

I stood up, taking her with me as I locked my lips over hers and kissed the heck out of her.

"You just made me the happiest man in the world," I exclaimed, refusing to let her go as I gently swung us in a circle. "My fiancée is having my baby!"

"I guess today is filled with lots of big things," she giggled.

"It sure is. And we're only a week away from you officially moving in with me."

"I think that was pretty much a done deal when you knocked me up. There's no way I'm doing all this by myself."

"I would never allow that to happen." I stopped swinging her and set her down, hoping I hadn't made her nauseous. I had no idea if she was experiencing any morning sickness, but I didn't want to make it worse if she was.

"You are my life, Paisley. You and this baby. There is not a single thing in the world that I wouldn't do for both of you. My only goal in life is to make sure you're happy and taken care of. I will be there for you every step of the way with this pregnancy. This is you and me together, baby. Nothing is going to stop us now."

"I love you, Maverick."

"I love you more."

# Thirty-Two

## Paisley

"You did not have to cook all of this for me," I said, sitting uncomfortably full at the table after devouring a four-course meal that Maverick made me for breakfast.

"It was my pleasure. Gotta feed you and my little squirt."

I scrunched my nose, not liking the nickname he was giving our unborn child. We had already been through muffin, nugget, bean, and peanut, none of which sounded right. It felt like we needed something other than *unborn child*, but we just hadn't found the right one yet.

"What's wrong with Squirt?" he asked, leaning over to load the dishwasher. "I think it's cute."

I popped a grape into my mouth and chewed, enjoying the view as his t-shirt stretched tightly over his muscular back.

"It reminds me of what *I* do and how you got me pregnant."

"Fair point."

He stood up and leaned against the counter, giving it some thought with his arms crossed over his chest.

"How about Cletus the Fetus?" he offered.

"Cletus? Do you want our kid to get bullied in kindergarten?" I got up and walked over to him, wrapping my arms around his waist.

"There's no way in hell that will happen. I'll take down the little snot licker before they have a chance."

"Easy there," I teased, running my hands down his chest. "There's no need for such violence. Give the kid a break; they can't even tie their shoes."

"True." He nodded his head as if this was an everyday kind of conversation to have. "What about Spawn?"

"No. I'm not referring to our baby as *spawn*."

He arched an eyebrow, questioning my veto.

"When I hear spawn, I think of demon spawn. No thanks." I shrugged my shoulders.

"Alright, I've got it," he said, rubbing his hands excitedly as I stepped to the side.

I tilted my head, waiting to hear the ridiculous nickname he would throw at me this time.

"Pumpkin."

As much as I wanted to hate it, I didn't. Maybe it was because the baby had been conceived in the fall, and I associated that with pumpkins, or maybe it was because I was craving pumpkin pie all the time. But something about it just fit.

"Pumpkin," I repeated, nodding my head in agreement. "I like it."

"Good. Then that's settled. Now let's go open presents. I got you something I think you're really going to like."

"Same," I said with a flirty smirk as I walked past him and headed to the living room.

************************************************

"I want to say I have a favorite, but I love them all," Maverick said, flipping through the photos I had printed for him from the boudoir session I had done with Calli. I sat there nervously chewing my nails as I waited for him to get to the black leather dominatrix ones.

I could tell the moment he did because his fingers stopped moving, and his eyes darkened. He shifted uncomfortably on the floor beside me, tugging at the fabric of his joggers as he slowly flipped through them. The last picture was the one Calli got a close-up of me with my finger slipping inside my pussy.

"Let's go," he said gruffly, setting the pictures to the side and standing up.

"But we didn't finish," I objected with a laugh as he bent down and tossed me over his shoulder, carrying me back to the bedroom.

"Maverick," I squealed, loving the way his fingers gripped my body before gently setting me on the bed. "We weren't done opening gifts."

"The rest can wait—trust me." He wiggled his eyebrows before pulling his shirt over his head and tossing it to the floor. His beautifully sculpted body was one of my favorite sights, and suddenly, I didn't care about the rest of the presents we hadn't opened yet. He was about to give me the gift that kept on giving.

152

# Thirty-Three

## Maverick

"I'm going to be a dad," I announced proudly to my parents, pulling Paisley into my side as we sat on the couch at their house. We were celebrating Christmas with them on New Year's Eve because they had been out of town for the holiday. Since Paisley was pregnant, we didn't see the need to go to any big parties and stay up late to watch the ball drop. I was getting ready to start the new year with a fiancée and a baby on the way, and nothing could top that.

"Oh my goodness," my mother said, immediately wiping the tears from her eyes. "Congratulations! I'm so happy for you guys!"

"Congratulations! That's wonderful news," my father replied before standing up to pull me into a hug. "I'm proud of you, son."

"Thanks, Dad."

"I can't believe it," my mom said, smiling proudly at us. "First, we find out that you two are getting married, and now that we're going to be grandparents. There are so many exciting things happening in our family and I just love it. Have you guys set a date for the wedding?"

"Not yet," Paisley answered, looking up at me briefly. "I wanted to have a spring wedding, but I worry that whatever dress I pick now won't fit then. I'm not sure whether it's a good idea to try to plan a wedding while being pregnant since so much can change so quickly."

"We could always get married now," I offered. I didn't want to put her on the spot, but at the same time, I couldn't stop the nagging feeling deep inside of me saying that I should marry her now. It wasn't that I worried something would go wrong and she would change her mind; it was that I couldn't wait another minute to make her my wife and spend forever with her.

"Like as in on your parent's couch right now?" she teased.

"No," I replied with a laugh. "But we could do a winter wedding that would still be beautiful, Paisley. And you wouldn't have to wait as long, so whatever dress you pick now would likely still fit. We could do something like Valentine's Day—"

She scrunched her nose and shook her head, forcing me to chuckle.

"Or not. The point is that we don't have to wait that long to get married. We can plan a perfect wedding and do it soon. That way, you don't have to stress over all the what-ifs, and I get to call you my wife sooner."

Paisley pulled her shoulders back and stared off into the distance as she thought about it.

"How about January 14th? That gives us two weeks to get things situated. I don't need a big wedding with all the bells and whistles. I can find a dress and take care of the little things during my downtime at work. Calli can make the food for the reception, and I'm sure I can ask Maggie to make the cake."

"I can do the photos," Mom offered, leaning forward as she hung onto every word.

"And if you're interested, I have a friend who has a large ranch with a gorgeous rustic barn that you guys could get married in." My dad wrapped an arm around my mom's shoulders, both of them looking happier than I'd seen them in a while.

I loved that they were as excited as we were but that they weren't being pushy or trying to tell us what to do.

"We can talk over things later and let you guys know," I said, squeezing her hand reassuringly. I didn't want her to feel rushed into making a decision on everything right now, especially if she had other ideas for what she wanted. There was a lot happening all at once, and I didn't want to create any unnecessary stress for her right now.

"Sounds lovely, dear. And Paisley, if there's anything we can do for you during your pregnancy, please don't hesitate to let us know."

"Thank you. I appreciate that."

I leaned into the couch, allowing my body to relax, knowing that everything in life was finally going in the right direction.

*************************

By the time we got home from my parents' house, it was late, and Paisley had gone straight to bed. She had insisted that she would stay up so we could ring in the new year together, but I felt better that she was getting the rest that she and the baby needed.

It still felt incredibly weird to say that we were having a baby, but I couldn't be happier.

Never in a million years did I see myself getting married and having a baby with a woman I had only been dating for a few months, but that was exactly what was happening. Who were we to try to intervene when fate was involved?

I finished cleaning up the mess in the kitchen before heading up to bed when I noticed a missed call from Jackson. We had been chatting back and forth for a few weeks through text messages as he was slammed with the holidays—both at work and with his family.

I pressed the play button and listened as the voicemail started.

*"Hey Maverick, sorry to call so late. We just wrapped up the end-of-year stuff we needed to get done, so I wanted to check in on our conversation. If your friend is still interested in a marketing position, please have her email her resume, and we'll take a look at it. I'll be in the office on Monday, but you can send it to HR and they'll get started on it. Let me know if you have any questions."*

My grin split across my face, knowing that there were more wonderful opportunities on the horizon. I couldn't wait for Paisley to wake up so I could tell her the good news.

# Thirty-Four

## Paisley

"What do you think about this one?" Calli asked, holding up a beautiful long-sleeved white dress with a sheer lace overlay.

My heart raced at the sight of it, admiring the beauty in the intricate details. I stepped forward, trying to see the price without letting her know.

As if already knowing what I was up to, she quickly covered the tag in her hand and cocked her head to the side as she pinned me with a look.

"Do you like it?" she pressed, still refusing to let go of the tag.

"I do…"

"But?"

"But you won't let me see how much it costs and I'm getting anxious about how expensive everything in here is," I whispered loudly to her without letting the sales lady by the register overhear us. "We're getting married and having a baby—both of which are already getting to be quite costly. I don't want to spend an absurd amount on a dress that I'm only going to wear once."

"Paisley, I say this with love—stop being a pain in the ass and just pick a dress."

I arched an eyebrow and placed a hand on my hip as I stared at her.

"It's not that easy."

"Yes, it is."

"I hate to break it to you, but I'm not just rolling in the dough. I don't have the luxury of buying whatever I want without having to worry about how much it costs."

Calli set the dress down and stepped in front of me, holding my hands in hers.

"I get that. And I wasn't going to say anything—because I was threatened not to—but you are already set up to have whatever dress in here you'd like. There's no cost to you. So literally all of them are free, Paisley. You just have to pick the one you want."

I shook my head, hoping it would dislodge the words that were stuck in my head.

"What are you talking about?"

"It's already been taken care of."

"How?"

"Your future in-laws made some arrangements. This is one of them. And since this is the best—and only," she whispered, "dress store in Whiskey Mountain, you have your pick. Whatever your heart desires."

My heart raced in my chest, beating wildly. It hadn't even been a full forty-eight hours since we announced our engagement to Maverick's parents and they were already moving mountains to make this work for us on such short notice.

"Can I still see how much it costs before I make a decision?" I asked.

I knew that it technically didn't matter to anyone else since I wasn't the one paying for it, but I wasn't going to take advantage of Maverick's parents' generosity. There was a big difference between the $200 dress I initially looked at compared to the $1500 dress I saw in the window before we walked in.

"No."

I frowned and tugged my lower lip between my teeth.

"Just follow your heart, Paisley. Which dress is calling your name?"

I sighed heavily, looking from the $200 one I had my mind set on to the one she was holding again. It was gorgeous, and it was what I imagined I would wear someday if I got married.

"That one." I pointed at it and felt my cheeks split into a grin as she smiled widely at me.

"Perfect. I'll take care of this, but while I'm doing that, it wouldn't hurt you to browse the bridesmaid dresses over there. I'll need some guidance on what you want me to wear since I'll be your maid of honor and all." She winked playfully but already knew she was going to be it.

I walked over and browsed the dresses on the rack, hating that I hadn't figured out any of the details for our wedding yet. Technically, it had only been a day since I agreed to marry Maverick in two weeks, but I was starting to reconsider moving so quickly with everything.

He had sent me out to do some shopping with Calli while he and Dylan took care of moving my stuff over to his house. Everyone was all hands on deck, ready to jump in and help however we needed, but I hated the feeling that I couldn't even stop for a few minutes to think about what I wanted. I needed to sit down and talk to Maverick, but I didn't want him to think that I was reconsidering marrying him. I wanted nothing more than to be his wife, but I didn't need the big wedding and stuff to make our marriage real.

I pushed a handful of dresses to the side, already ruling them out since they were sleeveless and short—not ideal for a winter wedding. There weren't a lot of options to choose from, and I wanted something that Calli would be comfortable in. We weren't having a big wedding, so I wasn't concerned with finding anyone else to be in it. Maverick had asked Dylan to be his best man, which worked well since Calli was my maid of honor.

I picked up a blush-colored dress that would look beautiful on Calli and checked the price tag. It wasn't as expensive as I had expected, but still, $120 for a dress she would only wear once was a bit much. I set it back on the rack and went to reach for another one when my phone rang. I pulled it out of my pocket and swiped my finger across the screen to answer it, not recognizing the phone number on the caller ID.

"Hello," I answered, tucking the phone between my ear and shoulder as I hung the dress up.

"Hi, may I please speak with Paisley?" a woman asked, her voice soft yet professional.

"Yes, this is she."

"Hi, Paisley. This is Bea, calling from Mason, Inc. We received your resume, and I wanted to touch base to see if we could set up a time for you to do an online interview."

"Oh my gosh, yes, hi!" I hated how high my voice squealed when I realized who I was speaking to. Maverick and I had talked about it after he got the voicemail from Jackson, and I sent in my resume right away, but it still surprised me to get her call. "That would be wonderful. Thank you."

"It's our pleasure. Mr. Mason mentioned that he wanted to schedule something as soon as possible as he has a position immediately available. Would you be available this afternoon at four pm?"

I glanced at my watch, noticing it was already after two. Calli and I had a few more errands we were planning to run, but I knew she would totally take a raincheck so I could do the interview.

"Yes. That sounds perfect."

"Wonderful. I will email you shortly with the details and the link so you can join the call. If you need anything in the meantime, please feel free to reach out to me."

"Thank you so much, Bea. I appreciate it."

"Not a problem. We'll see you at four."

I smiled as I hung up, feeling electricity in the air around me. Calli headed my way, her brows pulled in with curiosity as a garment bag hung over her arm.

"What's up?" she asked, tilting her head as she studied me.

"I just got off the phone with the company Maverick's friend works at—Mason, Inc. I have an interview today at four!"

"Oh my gosh! Paisley! That's amazing!"

"Thank you! Sorry, we'll have to wrap stuff up a little early."

"Don't be. We got the most important thing done today— finding you a dress."

"Thanks. I still can't believe his parents did that."

She smiled warmly and grabbed the dress I had been looking at before I took the call, hanging it over her arm on top of mine.

"What are you doing?" I asked, frowning as we headed toward the front door.

"Getting my dress."

My brow furrowed deeper, not understanding.

"I saw you looking at it, and you had this look in your eye. It's the one you get when you really love something. Then I saw you check the price and put it back, which confirmed that this is the right dress. So I'm getting it."

"Calli, you don't have to do that. We can find something less expensive," I said quietly through clenched teeth as I attempted to smile at the sales lady at the register.

"I don't *have* to do anything, Paisley. My best friend is getting married, and *this* is the dress I'm wearing to her wedding. Now stop fussing and let me have my joy."

"This is a beautiful dress," the saleswoman said, scanning the tag to ring it up. "Did you need shoes to go with it?"

"No, thank you. I already have some that will go perfectly," Calli answered.

I waited for Calli to finish paying, and then we walked out together, greeted by a cold rush of air.

"Do you have something to wear to your interview?" she asked, pressing the button to unlock her car.

"It's an online one," I said, not even thinking about what I should wear to it. "It's not an actual in-person one."

"No, but you still want to be dressed appropriately for it," she countered as we climbed in and got buckled. "We'll tackle the rest of the wedding stuff this week, but right now, we're going shopping for your new job."

"I don't even know that I'll get it." I laughed nervously. It wasn't like I had the experience they were looking for, so it was a long shot. Plus, I would be starting a new job pregnant and needing to take maternity leave before I even completed a year there—not that I had to disclose that information to them in the interview. But still, it felt wrong to lead them on and not let them know that I had some personal things that would be happening soon.

"You will get it because you're insanely talented and one of the best marketers I've ever met. You could sell free water and make a profit on it."

I rolled my eyes and laughed at her overly dramatic analogy.

"I don't want to go spend a bunch of money on clothes for a new job until I know for sure that I have it. Plus, I'll have to be smart about it since I'll have to transition to maternity clothes sooner rather than later."

"Well, how about we start with finding a new outfit for you to wear to the interview?" she offered.

"Deal. But can we *please* go to the thrift shop? It's giving me heartburn thinking about how much money we've spent already today."

"I think the heartburn *might* be from the six strips of bacon and four sausage links you had at breakfast, but yes, we can hit up Whiskey Savers. I was hoping to do some shopping there for maternity clothes, too, so we can multitask."

I leaned back in the passenger seat and wondered when things were going to feel calm again.

*******************************

I sat up straight in front of the computer screen, adjusting the tank top Calli had convinced me to buy for the interview. It felt weird to be wearing a sleeveless shirt during the middle of winter, but it went perfectly with the beige pencil skirt that was also on sale. The shirt was a darker brown with a polka dot print that matched the color of the skirt and screamed professional compared to the clothes I typically wore.

The screen changed as Bea and Mr. Mason entered the call,

their cameras turning on as my face popped up in a square alongside theirs.

"Hello, Paisley. Thank you for taking the time to meet with us today," Bea said warmly.

"Thank you so much for giving me the opportunity to interview for a position with Mason, Inc." I rubbed my hands nervously under the table as I struggled not to fidget or appear nervous. "It's an honor to be considered by such a prestigious company."

"The honor is ours," Mr. Mason said, clearing his throat.

I smiled and tried to breathe through the flush that was washing over my cheeks.

"We've reviewed your resume and reached out to a few of your previous employers," Bea said, getting straight to it. "Can you tell us a little more about your experience with Cravings?"

I nodded, hoping that I would be able to clearly articulate what I needed to since this was the closest job I had to actual advertising. I didn't want to stretch the truth about what I did for Calli, but I also didn't want to make Maverick look like an idiot for recommending someone who didn't have any real experience.

"Yes, um. Cravings is a restaurant that my best friend opened in Whiskey Mountain after moving to town to take care of her mother. I moved with her, not sure of what my role would be until after we got here." I cleared my throat and pinched the skin between my fingers to try to force myself to concentrate.

Mr. Mason's features changed suddenly, but I tried not to focus on that. If he were already unimpressed, then it would be pointless to continue with the interview. But I only had one chance to impress him, and I was determined not to waste it. I sat taller, pulled my shoulders back, and tried again.

"It was a big change moving from Miami to such a small town, but I quickly learned to navigate it. As I'm sure you saw on my resume, I worked as an executive assistant at a large advertising company in Miami. I already had some experience, just not directly in advertising."

They both nodded with Mr. Mason keeping his focus on me while Bea lowered her head and wrote something down on the notepad in front of her.

"When we got to Whiskey Mountain, I knew deep in my heart that I wanted to make my best friend's dream a reality. It was hard being new in town, but even harder trying to get a restaurant started from the ground up. Not only that, but the concept of her restaurant wasn't anything like what the locals were used to. It was a huge change, and she needed help getting started. I decided to take over the advertising for her, and before we knew it, her business skyrocketed."

I noticed a ghost of a smile on Mr. Mason's face as I continued talking.

"People were lining up before we opened, ready to be the first ones to see what would be on the menu that day. Calli, my best friend, changed it daily according to what her mother was craving that day. It was a fun twist that kept everyone interested and gave me an opportunity where to direct my marketing. Instead of just telling people that there was a new food place in town, I focused on why it was different and drove business through fear of missing out. No one knew when Calli would have something on the menu again, so there was this need to get it before it was gone. I created social media accounts for Cravings and constantly made teasers about what would be on the menu that day before we were open to drive interest. When people came into Cravings, I would have signs up asking them to follow us on social media for sneak peeks at what would be coming and to get exclusive deals. I made sure that there was a benefit for them coming into the restaurant, as well as having an online presence."

"That's quite creative," Mr. Mason said, nodding his head. "How is business going for Cravings now that it's been open for a while?"

"It's going very well. There's a line out the door constantly, and unfortunately for me, word of mouth has taken over as the new marketing tactic, so there's not as much of a need for marketing right now. I maintain the social media accounts and keep those active, which helps keep a steady line of traffic out the door. But honestly, I think Cravings would do just fine now that it's established, even without the social media presence. It's great to find new patrons, but that's kind of hard to focus on being in a small town when you don't get a lot of new people. The town regulars already know what to expect and are devoted customers by now."

"Have you guys thought about expanding due to the demand?"

I shook my head, feeling more relieved that I was getting in my element.

"No, I don't think that will ever be an option. Calli enjoys running her own business, but she's very dedicated to caring for her mother and doesn't wish to take on more than she can handle right now. Expanding the business would be both expensive and time-consuming, which would have a negative effect on her current business. If we were to expand and start a second one, there wouldn't be as high of demand since there would be more access to it, which would also make it harder to recoup the costs of adding a second location."

"Very well said," Mr. Mason commented. "I agree. I think her current business model is quite successful."

 "Where do you see yourself now with the company, since you've stated that your role with marketing has more or less come to an end?" Bea asked, looking up from her notepad.

"Honestly, I'm not sure. I still help out there, but more so up front, working the register and taking over wherever Calli needs me. While I wish there were more of a need for marketing, I'm thankful that her business is doing so well not to need it."

They both nodded and exchanged a look that I had a hard time reading. I tried to ignore the negative thoughts running through my head about how I wasn't cut out for this.

Mr. Mason leaned forward and steepled his hands in front of him on his desk, looking down before lifting his eyes to meet mine.

"We have an opening for a marketing consultant that I think you would be a great candidate for," he said, sending a wave of shivers over my skin. "One of the hardest aspects of marketing is thinking outside of the box, but you've proved you're very capable of doing just that. You took a business from the ground up and got it to the point it can stand on its own without needing any additional marketing. That's a feat in itself and speaks volumes to your abilities."

I breathed in deeply, letting the air out slowly through my mouth as I tried to calm myself.

"If you're interested in moving forward, I would like to schedule an interview with our New York office as soon as possible. We're looking to fill that position as quickly as possible and have it narrowed down to a handful of candidates. Most of the interviews are taking place tomorrow; however, I can add you to the schedule for Wednesday if that works better for your schedule," Bea offered.

"New York?" I blurted out, trying to keep the shock off of my face.

"Yes. This position would be for our New York location. Would that be a problem?"

I pressed my lips together to keep from blurting out a

response that I wouldn't be able to take back.

"Um, no. Not at all," I lied, wringing my hands together in my lap.

"Wonderful." Bea smiled and wrote something else down before turning to her computer and staring at the screen. Her hand moved over the mouse as she clicked it rapidly, then stopped and looked at me. "We can do tomorrow at three thirty or Wednesday at ten AM. Do either of those work for you?"

"Wednesday would be great," I replied, feeling a sheen of sweat cover my skin as I thought about how to navigate all of this.

"Perfect. I've got you down for Wednesday at ten. I'll send over the details in an email, however, please reach out if you need anything in the meantime."

"Thank you."

"It was a pleasure meeting with you, Paisley." Mr. Mason smiled and then his camera turned off, ending the call.

I pushed away from the table, staring at the blank screen as I wondered what I had just gotten myself into.

# Thirty-Five

## Maverick

Paisley was acting differently after she finished her interview, which made me hesitant to ask her how it went. I was excited for her and knew that Jackson would likely give her a chance because of our friendship, but I didn't expect him to just give her a job. At the same time, I also didn't want to accept that he was possibly a dick to her because then I would have to kick his ass. Nobody messed with my girl or hurt her feelings—not on my watch.

I started on dinner, giving her time to herself until she was ready to talk. I had learned enough about Paisley to know when she needed space and when to push her. Now wasn't the time for pushing. If anything, now was the time to pamper and take care of her however she needed.

The food was just about done by the time she came into the kitchen, wearing her favorite loose pajamas.

"Dinner is almost ready," I said, leaning in to kiss her cheek.

She smiled, but it didn't last longer than a few seconds. It was killing me to know that she was upset about something but not what it was.

I worked on taking the lasagna out of the oven and finished the garlic bread while Paisley sat down at the table and fidgeted with the glass of water I had poured for her. I tried to keep my mood light and not focus on the dread that was threatening to take over me as I worried about what was going on.

I served each of us and then set the plates on the table, taking a seat across from her.

"It smells delicious. Thank you for cooking," she said softly, cutting into the lasagna with her fork.

"My pleasure."

I wanted to add that it was a celebratory dinner, but given that I didn't know how the interview went, I didn't want to stick my foot in my mouth. The tension in the air between us was thick, nearly suffocating me.

We ate in silence for a few minutes, neither of us bothering to look at each other. I didn't want her to see the worry on my face, nor did I want to stress her out further than she already was.

"I can't do this," she blurted out, letting her fork fall to the plate.

I set mine down and gripped the sides of the table, preparing myself for whatever she was about to say. My heart raced, palms sweating as I waited for her to break my heart in some way or another.

"I'm sorry," she continued, wiping the tears that started rolling down her face.

"You don't have to apologize for anything, Paisley," I said softly, reaching over and placing my hand over hers. I had no idea what she couldn't do anymore, but I knew for certain that I wasn't letting her go.

"Yes, I do. I can't do all of this, Maverick." She pulled her hand away and threw them in the air. "It's all too much. The wedding. A baby. The interviews. New York. I can't deal with all of this at once."

"What are you talking about? What's in New York?"

"The job I'm interviewing for with Mason, Inc. They asked

me to continue with the interview process, but the position would be at their New York office."

I leaned back in my chair, suddenly understanding what the problem was.

"I can't do this, Maverick. There are too many decisions that I'm supposed to make without having any time to think through them. Between planning the wedding and having a baby—that's overwhelming enough. To add on a possible new job that's thousands of miles away—it's just too much. I can't do this right now."

"What are you saying, Paisley."

She looked down at the table as her tears continued rolling down her face. I knew what was coming, but that didn't help soften the blow once she started speaking.

"I want to take a break. I can't marry you right now, Maverick. I need time to think about what I want and what all of this means."

# Thirty-Six

## Paisley

The hurt look on Maverick's face was worse than anything I had ever seen before in my life, and it was because I knew that *I* was the reason it was there. *I* had hurt him.

"I'm sorry," I apologized, hoping he would hear the sincerity in my voice with the words I spoke. "I'm not trying to hurt you. I just need a moment to figure things out and try to catch my breath. I can't *breathe* right now, Maverick. I'm suffocating and don't know how to fix any of this."

He worked his jaw back and forth as he continued his grip on the side of the table. I could see his knuckles turning white as he struggled to control himself.

"What is that you want, Paisley? If you could have the perfect life, what would it look like?"

"That's not a fair question," I objected, frustrated that he couldn't understand.

"Yes, it is. You know what you want. Deep in your heart, you know what you want. I'm asking you to tell me what that is. In a perfect world, what would yours look like?"

I sat back in my chair, unsure of how to answer him.

"It would be me and you. Our baby." I swallowed hard, trying to work up the courage to say the rest. "But at the same time, I want a career. I want to have it all. Being a mom and happily married to the love of my life while also having a career that I love. A job that is meaningful and brings me the same joy that you do. But I can't have both, Maverick. And it kills me that this is all happening at the same time because I don't want to have to pick. I know we didn't plan to have a baby, and I don't know that we would still be getting married if I wasn't pregnant. It's just like the timing is all wrong."

"I had your ring before I ever knew you were pregnant," he said softly, looking up at me as his grip on the table softened. "I knew I wanted to marry you before you told me you were pregnant. Our engagement had nothing to do with you getting knocked up, Paisley."

"I know," I said with a heavy sigh. "But still, this is all happening and I have a once-in-a-lifetime chance at my dream job, yet I can't take it."

"Why not?"

"How in the world do you think I could?" I asked, laughing in disbelief at his delusion. "We live here, Maverick. You're taking over your dad's business. Everything is set up here, I can't just up and move to New York because I have a chance to work for Mason, Inc."

He pushed away from the table and paced the space in front of the island for a few as he ran a hand through his hair.

"We'll move to New York," he said matter-of-factly.

"What?" My brows pulled together as I stood up and blocked his path so he would stop pacing. "What in the world are you talking about?"

"I'll move to New York with you. We'll get married when and how you want—if you still want to marry me. We'll raise our baby in the city."

"Maverick, it's not that easy. You can't just up and move your entire life for me."

"Yes, I can. Paisley, life isn't worth living without you. You give me something to live for, so if your happiness comes from taking a job in New York, then you can bet your ass I will make that happen."

I shook my head, feeling dizzy from how fast things were moving again.

"What about your business? What about taking over your dad's business? You already got everything settled with that. You can't just walk away."

"Sure I can. I have cousins who can take over. It'll still stay in the family."

"Maverick," I said softly, reaching for him. "You can't do this."

"I can and I will. I wasn't lying when I told you that *you* are my life, Paisley. We do this together. If this is what you want, I'm fully on board."

I pulled in a deep breath and slowly exhaled it.

"I don't even know if I'll get the job," I said shakily.

"Either way, my only goal in life is to make you happy. You tell me what you want and need, and I'll make it happen. If you want to put off getting married for a while, that's fine, too. I don't want to cause any unnecessary stress for you, Paisley."

"I appreciate that. I'm sorry I freaked out. It's just a lot all at once, and I feel like I'm drowning under the weight of all the decisions I'm supposed to make."

He grabbed me gently, pulling me into his arms where he held me. I breathed in his soft scent, allowing it to calm my senses the way it always did.

"I still want to marry you," I said softly. "I picked a dress today and everything."

"I can't wait to see it. But Paisley, trust me when I say that I will wait as long as you need me to."

"Thank you." I leaned closer to him and listened to his heartbeat.

"When do you find out about the job?" he asked softly, releasing his hold on me as he guided me back to my seat so we could eat dinner.

"I have a second interview on Wednesday with the New York office. Bea, the HR manager, sent me an email with the information for it, as well as to confirm that they would make a decision by Friday. They're trying to fill the position quickly."

"Well, it sounds like the one today went well if you're moving on to the next round."

"It did," I said, taking a bite of my bread and nodding. "They were both very nice, and I felt excited about the possibility of working with them when they talked about the company and the current projects they're working on."

"I bet you'll get it," he said, winking before taking a drink of water. "Life in New York is going to be fun."

"We don't have to rush into anything yet," I replied softly. "Let's see how the next interview goes before we start making any big plans."

# Thirty-Seven

## Maverick

I was waiting on pins and needles for a call from Paisley once I knew her interview would be over. It had been over an hour since it started, but I had no idea how long it should take.

"Have you heard anything?" Calli asked, coming to check on me as I sat impatiently in a booth, poking at the food I hadn't bothered to eat yet. I had spent the day running errands in town, including finally meeting up with Mr. Crawford to settle what I owed from when Paisley and I stayed there.

"Not yet." I let my head fall back, wishing I could somehow have Paisley call me with an update.

Just then, the door to Cravings opened, and she walked in.

Seeing her in another one of those tight skirts made my body temperature skyrocket as I tried not to get turned on by how sexy she looked. Now wasn't the time nor the place, but still, there was something incredibly sexy about a plain black skirt that hugged her curves just right, mixed with a somewhat sheer shirt that showed her bra.

"Hey," I said, getting up and rushing over to her. "How did it go?"

She smiled at me and then at Calli, who joined us.

"It went well," she replied with a smile as she exhaled

heavily. "I got the job."

"What? That's amazing!" I grabbed her and spun her around, trying my best not to make her nauseous, but I couldn't contain my excitement. "I thought they weren't deciding until Friday?"

I stopped moving and set her back down, allowing her a moment to fix her shirt that I had accidentally pulled loose from the skinny belt wrapped around her waist.

"They were, but said that they knew I was right for the job so they offered it to me on the spot at the end of the interview."

"Congratulations! That's amazing!" Calli said cheerfully.

"Yes, congratulations, my love. I'm so proud of you."

"Thank you, but I turned it down."

Calli and I stepped back at the same time, both of our jaws dropping.

"What do you mean you turned it down?" I asked, my brows pinched together.

"I thanked them for the opportunity but told them my life is in Whiskey Mountain."

"Paisley," I said, struggling to get my words out. "I told you, I will go wherever you go."

"I know, but it's not just that. I don't want to rush off to something new and exciting without giving my all to what I already have here. My life is here, Maverick. In Whiskey Mountain. My best friend is here. My *mom* is here. I can't just walk away from that, especially when I think about what all you would be walking away from for me. It just didn't feel right, so I turned it down."

I sat down at the table, unsure how to process all of this.

"Are you sure that's what you want?" Calli asked softly as they both sat down and joined me.

"It is. I gave it a lot of thought and considered all options. While it would be nice to have a job doing something I love, I would rather do something that makes me happy. And that's being here with you guys. I want to be a mom and have our babies grow up together. I don't want to be miles away, only talking to each other on FaceTime when we get the chance."

"We can make things work," I offered softly, not wanting her to give up so easily.

"Things already work," she countered, covering my hand with hers. "Don't you see that? We have everything we need right here. While the job sounded amazing, I would miss out on what truly makes me happy by going after it."

"But, Paisley…"

"No, Maverick. You have always told me that life is about finding something to live for, and I found that. I found you. You're willing to go the extra mile to make my dreams come true, but they already have."

"I'm going to get back up there since we're getting a line, but we'll talk later," Calli said, excusing herself from the table.

"Are you sure about this?" I asked, squeezing her hand gently. "I don't want you to give up on something you wanted so badly."

"I'm more than sure about it. I think I knew all along what I wanted, I was just overwhelmed with too many decisions and got freaked out. It was like I had a sudden sense of clarity when they offered me the job and I've never felt more certain about anything in my life. I know what I want, and it's you and this baby. Our life together. Here. Forever."

"Okay," I said softly, nodding my head in agreement. "Well, I guess I'll have some calls to make then."

"Why's that?"

"Well, I was being proactive with us moving to New York, so I already started talking to my dad about selling the business to my cousin. I also talked to a realtor who is getting ready to list the house."

Her eyebrows shot up to her forehead.

"Maverick!"

"I was fully on board with moving, Paisley. I wanted you to know that by being a team player and getting stuff done. I worried that if I dragged my feet even a little, you would worry that I wasn't serious about it."

"I can't believe you did that!"

"It's okay. I can talk to my dad and tell him not to do anything. I'll make a call real quick before the agent makes the listing. It's all easy to take care of."

She smiled and shook her head at me.

"What are you doing with the rest of your day?" I asked, pushing my plate to her so she could eat.

She picked up a chip and popped it into her mouth.

"I'm going to run some errands."

"Yeah? What kind?"

"The wedding planning kind."

She smiled widely, making my heart flutter.

# Thirty-Eight

## Paisley

"Are you ready?" Calli asked, fixing my veil as I looked at myself in the full-length mirror.

"I am."

"You look beautiful," Mom said, pulling me into a tight hug. I was happy that she was having a good day, even if she might not remember any of it later. She and Calli were the closest thing I had to family, so it meant a lot to me that they were there with me on my special day. But still, there was a sadness pulling inside my chest that my real mother never got to see this moment since she passed when I was little.

"Thank you." I leaned in and gently kissed her cheek.

"Alright, ladies, it's show time," Dylan said, popping into the doorway and smiling at us. "I'll walk Mom to her seat, then come back for Calli."

I nodded, feeling butterflies swarm in my stomach as I took one last look in the mirror. Calli stood next to me, lifting her cell phone to get a selfie of us on my wedding day.

"No crying," I warned, noticing the tears in her eyes.

"You either."

"Deal," I sniffled, gently wiping at mine to keep from smearing my makeup.

I walked over to get a tissue, thankful I had a few minutes

to get myself together. Dylan came for Calli a few minutes later, leaving me to myself.

I didn't have anyone to walk me down the aisle, but it didn't bother me. It was a small wedding, and I was more than comfortable walking by myself. It wasn't about having someone to give me away as much as it was about having someone who was waiting to spend their life with me.

The music started playing, my cue to head out. I admired the effort and attention to detail that Maverick's family had made in decorating the barn for the wedding. I had given them some color swatches that I liked that matched the bouquets and Calli's dress, and they handled the rest. From the flowers lining the blush-colored runner to the soft lights strung across the wooden beams, it was perfect and romantic.

My head was down as I focused on not tripping over my own two feet, but when I looked up, I found the most incredibly gorgeous man smiling at me. I felt my cheeks split as I smiled back, walking faster to get to him.

"You look incredible," he said softly as I finally reached him, neither of us able to keep our hands off each other.

"Thank you. So do you."

He smiled and leaned in to kiss me before the officiant cleared his throat to remind us of his presence.

I giggled and looked away from Maverick before I got myself in trouble.

"Ladies and gentlemen, we are gathered here today to join Paisley Brooks and Maverick Thompson in holy matrimony. Every one of us has a deep longing to love and be loved; however, your marriage today is a public affirmation of the bonding that has already begun. Today is a day of celebration. We celebrate the love the two of you hold in your hearts as you embark upon the journey to share the rest of your lives together. If anyone has any objections, speak now, or forever hold your peace."

The room was silent as Maverick and I looked at each other, knowing no one would have any reason to object.

"Paisley and Maverick have written their own vows, which they will now read to each other."

I smiled as Maverick nodded for me to go first. I had mine memorized, but when I looked at him, I couldn't remember a single thing I had written down.

"I love you," I said with more certainty than anything before. "I'm head over heels, absolutely in love with you, Maverick. I can't promise to be the perfect wife, but I do promise to always try my best. I will love you unconditionally and will always do everything in my power to make you happy. We might fight and disagree, but I will always be on your side. Your demons will be my demons, and we'll conquer them together. I want nothing more than to be your wife and bring you the same joy that you bring to my life. I love you more than words will ever be able to express."

"I love you too, Paisley," he said softly with a grin.

"Oh—and I won't cheat on you, nor will I hold you responsible for the stuff you do in my dreams," I added, feeling self-conscious when I heard people chuckling. "For the most part. You have done some messed up stuff in my dreams."

"I promise to do my best to stop messing up in your dreams," he replied with a sneaky grin, saying it loud enough for me to hear but not everyone else.

"Paisley, I love you more than I love anything. You are my world, and I will live the rest of my life making sure you have everything you want and need. I will never take you for granted or forsake you. I will always respect and honor you, making sure that you feel safe, loved, and secure in our marriage. I will be the best husband and father I can be and will do my best to learn along the way. My life is devoted to loving you and making sure you know how much you mean to me. I promise to take care of you and to do everything in my power to make you happy."

"You're going to be a wonderful dad," I agreed, squeezing his hands.

The officiant looked between us, making sure we were done before he continued.

"Do you, Paisley, take Maverick to be your lawfully wedded husband? To live together in matrimony, to love, comfort, honor, and keep him in sickness and health, from this day forward, as long as you both shall live?"

"I do."

"Do you, Maverick, take Paisley to be your lawfully wedded wife? To live together in matrimony, to love, comfort, honor, and keep her in sickness and health, from this day forward, as long as you both shall live?"

"I do."

"I now pronounce you man and wife. You may kiss your bride."

Everyone clapped and cheered as Maverick wrapped his arm around my waist and lowered his mouth to mine, placing the most tender kiss against my lips.

I wanted nothing more than to take my husband back to our room and celebrate our wedding, but we still had to get through the reception. I giggled as he deepened the kiss, pushing him away gently before things could get too out of hand.

"You're officially Mrs. Thompson," he said, his voice low in my ear.

"And I couldn't be happier."

I stepped away as we turned and faced our audience, happy faces greeting us as they stood with tears in their eyes and continued to cheer for us.

"Let's get this party started," Maverick said, leading me down the aisle as rice was tossed in the air, falling lightly around us.

# Thirty-Nine

## Maverick

I held my wife tightly as we danced our first dance, followed by the next ten. I wasn't ready or willing to give her up, even when my father asked to cut in and have a dance with the bride.

The reception was going smoothly, with Calli knocking it out of the park with the food and Paisley constantly having a smile on her face. My mom had done a great job with capturing plenty of pictures until I had to tell her to stop so she could enjoy herself. Everyone had gone out of their way to ensure everything was perfect, even with the last-minute planning.

I was standing in line at the bar for a glass of water when I felt someone's hand on my shoulder. I turned slightly, expecting it to be my dad or Dylan, but was surprised to see Jackson standing there.

"What? No fucking way," I said, turning around and clapping my arm around him in a hug. "What are you doing here?"

"We would have been here sooner, but the weather got bad on the way up. Sorry to miss the ceremony, but hopefully we aren't too late for the reception."

"Not at all. I'm glad you made it."

"I wouldn't miss it for the world."

I chuckled and shook my head, wondering what could have changed the hard exterior I used to know. The old Jackson that I went to school with would never have stepped away from work long enough to maintain a friendship, let alone drive hours to come to a friend's wedding he hadn't seen in years. But then a beautiful woman stepped out from beside him, and everything made sense.

"Thank you for coming. It's really great to see you."

"Thank you for the invite. We can't wait to meet your beautiful bride," the woman said as Jackson reached back and wrapped his arm around her waist, pulling her into his side.

"This is Emily. Emily, this is Maverick."

"Nice to meet you," I said, extending my hand to shake hers. "Paisley is right over—"

I turned to look for her when I felt her hand wrap around me as she snuck up behind me.

"Right here," she said happily, tucking herself into my side.

"It's nice to officially meet you," Jackson said, shaking her hand. "Congratulations."

"Thank you."

I took a moment to allow the happiness to overflow as Emily and Paisley introduced themselves to each other.

"We won't keep you guys. We just wanted to say hi," Emily said, starting to pull Jackson away.

"Before we go, I did want to give you a wedding gift," Jackson said, stopping her as he handed me a card.

"Thank you. We appreciate it." I lowered my head in thanks.

"It's our pleasure. But if I'm being honest, I do have a

selfish reason for being here."

"Oh yeah? What's that?" I cocked my head to the side and studied him.

"I came to offer Paisley a job."

She gasped softly beside me as she leaned in to hear him.

"I understand how hard it would be to move to New York when your life is clearly in Whiskey Mountain. I don't blame you for not wanting to start over when everything is already established here. So, I did some thinking and figured out a way to make things work for everyone."

"Okay," Paisley said, her voice uncertain.

"I have been very intrigued by how you managed to get a business off the ground so quickly and realized that we have an opportunity to continue that success, but on a small-town level. After doing some research, I found that there aren't any advertising companies here in Whiskey Mountain, which is where I come in."

We all took a deep breath and waited for him to continue before letting it out.

"I would like to set up business in Whiskey Mountain, and in doing so, I would like you to lead our branch here. Since this is a new initiative, I don't have an office for you to report to, but I thought we could start with a remote position. You could work from home or wherever you're most comfortable working. I'll pay for any operating expenses you need to get started and send down one of our IT techs to get you set up in our systems. You'll handle the local business here and report to Sugarplum Falls once a quarter for administrative meetings when needed. The salary can be negotiated, but if you're interested, I would like to officially offer you the position."

I stepped back, gently pushing Paisley forward so she could talk to Jackson.

"I don't know what to say," she whispered, shaking her head. "This feels like a dream."

"I can assure you it's not," I said with a laugh, resting my hand on her shoulder.

"I believe we could work well together and that starting a branch in Whiskey Mountain could be very profitable," Jackson assured her. "It would be my honor to bring you on board and have you take charge of this."

"Well, in that case, I accept."

Jackson smiled and accepted the hug she offered before leading Emily away to give Paisley and me a moment.

"Congratulations," I said, pulling her into a tight hug. "I'm so proud of you."

"I can't believe it. It's so surreal."

"Good things happen to those who deserve it. And you, my love, deserve all the best."

"So do you, my *husband*."

"Say it again," I urged, lowering my mouth to her neck and nibbling the area below her ear that drove her crazy.

"Husband."

"God, I can't wait to fuck you and have you scream that for the whole world to hear."

"What are you waiting for? Let's get this wedding night started."

She giggled as I picked her up, tossed her over my shoulder, and carried her through the barn and out the doors. Tonight was the first night of the rest of our lives, and I was determined to make sure my *wife* had everything she could ever ask for.

**********************************

Are you looking for more small-town romance? Be sure to check out the Beaumont Creek series and get ready for some smoking-hot firefighters!

Just One Time (Beaumont Creek Book 1)

https://books2read.com/u/3G52zK

Wanna hang out and chat books? Come find me in my Facebook reader group!

Samantha Baca's Smutties:

https://www.facebook.com/groups/2945710968775398/

# <u>Other Books By Samantha</u>

## <u>The Haven Brook Series</u>
## <u>(small-town romantic suspense):</u>

'Til Death Do Us Part (Haven Brook Book 1)

https://books2read.com/u/m2RJNR


The Cradle Will Fall (Haven Brook Book 2)

https://books2read.com/u/b6O0QE


The Ties That Bind (Haven Brook Book 3)

https://books2read.com/u/mqgoz8


A Very Haven Christmas (Haven Brook Book 4- Novella)

https://books2read.com/u/mvqGjj


Three Strikes, You're Gone (Haven Brook Book 5)

https://books2read.com/u/mvqL2z

## <u>The Dark Shadows Trilogy</u>
## <u>(romantic suspense)</u>

Five Steps Ahead (Dark Shadows Book 1)

https://books2read.com/u/38Q0gO


Ten Seconds Too Late (Dark Shadows Book 2)

https://books2read.com/u/3JRgVB


Against The Clock (Dark Shadows Book 3)

https://books2read.com/u/m2YwoR


## <u>The Stone Creek Series</u>
## <u>(small-town- novellas)</u>

Chocolate Covered Mistletoe (Stone Creek Book 1)

https://books2read.com/u/3LRk9N


Candy Coated Promises (Stone Creek Book 2)

https://books2read.com/u/mldP5Y


Pumpkin Spiced Possibilities (Stone Creek Book 3)

https://books2read.com/u/bojdwV

# <u>Beaumont Creek Series</u>
# <u>(small town)</u>

Just One Time (Beaumont Creek Book 1)

https://books2read.com/u/3G52zK


Second Chances (Beaumont Creek Book 2)

https://books2read.com/u/4Aj6Z0


Third Time's The Charm (Beaumont Creek Book 3)

https://books2read.com/u/b5lEyG


Four-ever Single (Beaumont Creek Book 4)

https://books2read.com/u/4j5jMX


Fifth Wheel (Beaumont Creek Book 5)

https://books2read.com/u/4XwKwa

## **<u>Whiskey Mountain Series</u>**
## **<u>(small-town- novellas)</u>**

Something To Talk About

https://books2read.com/u/4X62ag


Something To Think About

https://books2read.com/u/3GWAan


Something To Believe In

https://books2read.com/u/3yVzgB


Something To Live For

https://books2read.com/u/mllEOP


## **<u>Sugarplum Falls Series</u>**
## **<u>(Holiday Novellas- can be read as standalone)</u>**


Blame It On The Mistletoe
https://books2read.com/u/bw1rqe

Blame It On The Eggnog
https://books2read.com/u/38PPY6

Blame It On The Candy Canes
https://books2read.com/u/31DNo7

## Blame It On The Blizzard
https://books2read.com/u/b6z6XE

## Blame It On The Reindeer
https://books2read.com/u/baLAG6

## Blame It On The Carols
https://books2read.com/u/me8E9z

## Blame It On The Lattes
https://books2read.com/u/mB1E2A

## Blame It On The Secret Santa
https://books2read.com/u/mY9dGY

# **<u>Standalone Books</u>**

## One Last Wish

https://books2read.com/u/mqg7D9

## Finding Love In Apartment 2C (novella)

https://books2read.com/u/bze9aZ

## Cocky Counsel: A Hero Club Novel

https://books2read.com/u/31Kzkn

## All Is Fair In Food And War (novella)

https://books2read.com/u/bp8qjX

# **Holiday Books**
# **(novellas)**

Snow Place To Go

https://books2read.com/u/4A560N

A Very Merry Kissmas

https://books2read.com/u/bPDgy7

A Christmas Wish

https://books2read.com/u/4EKXpE

Holiday Hijinks

https://books2read.com/u/4DP6Ze

# <u>Acknowledgments</u>

As with every book I write, I'll never stop thanking my loyal readers for their constant love and support. Without you guys, there would be no reason to write—other than to get these pesky words and characters out of my head. You all are the real MVPs, and I'm eternally grateful for you.

I would like to say a huge thank you to my alpha readers for always going above and beyond for me every step of the way. You know my books and writing style so well now that you keep me on my toes and make sure I'm writing something I'll truly love and won't try to delete at the end. Amanda, Valerie, and Claire—thank you for being so fabulous. I appreciate you!

I couldn't do any of this without the additional help of my beta readers! You ladies are the fresh eyes that I need, and your excitement for each book is what keeps me going. You also know me and my style well by now, which is greatly appreciated as it keeps things moving smoothly, and we can focus on how to make the book even better. Malissa, Jackie, and Azucena, I will always be thankful for your help and our friendship!

There's a lot that goes into writing and publishing a book, but this would be so much harder without the constant love and support of my family. From day one, they've been right beside me, cheering me on. I could never fully express my gratitude for everything you all do for me. Thank you for pushing me to chase after my dreams!

To my ARC readers—you guys are the best. Thank you for taking a chance on my books if you're new to my work, and thank you for sticking around if you've been with me for a while. It's wild to think some of us have been together on this for over four years!

My dear sweet husband, thank you for being the biggest Dick I've ever known. Your love and devotion are what drive everything in my world, and I hope that you will always know how much I love and appreciate you.

And as always, I hope that my sweet girls will continue to follow their dreams and see what the future holds. The world is yours, my loves.

If you've made it this far through the acknowledgments, thank you! Be sure to check out my Other Books By Samantha Baca page and check out some of my other steamy romance series. If you're so inclined, join me in my reader group on Facebook! I would really love to have you there!

# About the Author

Samantha lives in the southwest with her husband and two small children after abandoning her childhood dream of living in a cabin in Colorado when she found that she couldn't afford to live there and was deathly allergic to the woods. When she's not writing, she's usually spouting off sarcastic remarks while drinking wine out of a coffee mug to look like a functional adult while chasing down her toddlers. She enjoys spending time with her family, watching reruns of Friends, and the 24/7 flow of coffee that can be found in her veins. Be sure to follow her on social media for updates on what she's working on.

You can find her here:

Facebook: https://www.facebook.com/AuthorSamanthaBaca

Instagram: https://instagram.com/author_samantha_baca

Goodreads: http://www.goodreads.com/authorsamanthabaca

Facebook Reader Group:

https://www.facebook.com/groups/2945710968775398/

Webpage: https://authorsamanthabaca.wordpress.com

Newsletter: http://eepurl.com/g0NcSj